Micah has been working against the conclave from the inside for decades, and the time has finally come to make a move. The problem is that the other conclave members are suspicious, and when Micah steps in to save a hero, he has to run.

Constantine left the conclave a while ago, and he never regretted it. When he's sent to pick up Micah, who he knows is a spy for the fallen heroes, he's relieved to see the man isn't hurt.

But their fight isn't over. The end has finally come for the conclave, but the transition won't be easy, and they have to deal with the old conclave members before a new group can take their place. Luckily, they have allies — and it's all thanks to Micah.

Constantine is in awe of what Micah has done. The more time they spend together, the more he falls for him, and he can hardly believe it when Micah falls for him, too.

But their fight is just beginning, and the entire supernatural community is at risk. Constantine and Micah want a future together, but the possibility that one or both of them won't make it to the end is high.

Can their love survive the last fight?

Like Changes
Copyright © 2022 Catherine Lievens
ISBN: 978-1-4874-3578-3
Cover art by Angela Waters

Published by eXtasy Books Inc

Look for us online at:
www.eXtasybooks.com

LIKE CHANGES
VIKINGS 6

BY

CATHERINE LIEVENS

CHAPTER ONE

M icah could never completely relax, not even when he was in his suite of rooms. He was still at the conclave home base, which meant anything could happen at any time.

The other conclave members wouldn't visit his private space, just like he would never visit theirs, but there was still the possibility of them noticing things, and he didn't have the energy to face any of them right now.

He sighed and checked the time. He had a meeting with them in only a few minutes, and he wasn't looking forward to it. Still, the reason for the meeting made him smile.

The fallen heroes were finally rising. It was something he'd been working toward for years, and he was glad the time had finally come. It put him in an awkward place, and his life would be forfeit if the conclave found out what he was doing, but he was convinced, and he wouldn't back down.

One way or another, the conclave would change, and the conclave members who'd twisted the conclave's mission and made it what it was now would pay.

Even though Micah was happy about what was happening, he wasn't looking forward to listening to the other conclave members screaming and yelling for an hour. They were pissed after the video the fallen heroes had sent to the heroes, and they'd want revenge. The problem was that no one knew where the fallen heroes were located, and Micah hoped things would stay that way. Mordred and his people needed to stay safe if they wanted to be able to help when it came to the conclave.

Micah pushed himself out of the comfortable armchair he'd been sitting in with a sigh. It was one of the things he'd miss when he had to leave, and he had no doubt he would leave eventually. Hopefully Micah would be able to move his furniture and his things, but if he couldn't, he'd deal with it. He'd always known this time would come, and he'd made sure not to leave anything he couldn't abandon in his conclave rooms.

After visiting the bathroom, he headed out. The conclave always met in the conclave room, where they also held the trials against traitors and the general meetings when something big happened, and this *was* big. They'd talk to each other before doing so with the heroes, but Micah already knew what would be said. He'd been working with the other conclave members for a few hundred years, even though he was the youngest of them. He knew all of them as if they were part of his family, and he supposed that in a way, they were.

No one could choose their family, and this wasn't any different.

Sometimes Micah wondered if he was the only one who could see what was happening and what the conclave had become. Was he really the only person who wanted to change it back to what it had been before?

But it was useless to ask himself that question, especially now.

He left his rooms and headed toward the conclave room for the meeting. Once it was over, he'd contact Mordred and let him know what had happened. The meeting had been called because of the video the fallen heroes had put out there, and Micah was curious. He already knew most of the conclave would want the fallen heroes to be killed. Unfortunately, they were a bunch of bloodthirsty people, especially when their power and authority were in question.

He could hear the yelling even before he reached the room.

2

He sighed heavily, but even though he wanted to turn around and go back to his rooms, he forged forward. Running away from this meeting wouldn't help. If anything, it would make things even harder.

Not all conclave members trusted each other. They all had a similar weight when it came to power and authority, but with Micah being the youngest, he usually had to go along with what the older members wanted. More than that, it was a majority problem. The conclave had seven members, and while only three were truly bad, the others often went along with whatever those wanted to keep the peace, as well as what they'd gained by becoming conclave members.

They'd gotten used to being rich and having power over heroes and most of the supernatural world. They didn't want that to change, and it was easier to ignore problems and act as if nothing bad was happening. That made Micah angry, and he'd thought about leaving the conclave several times, but he was needed. He was a traitor, and he didn't care. He gave every bit of information he could to Mordred and the fallen heroes, and they used it to save lives. Micah could never be sorry about that, but he knew how much danger he was in every day. Something was going to break, and he suspected it would happen soon, especially now that the fallen heroes were finally moving forward.

When he entered, he barely managed to hide his wince. Verne was in the middle of the room, screaming that this — whatever *this* was — was unacceptable. Micah had no idea what he was talking about, although he could easily imagine. Verne's face was red, and if he'd been mortal, he might have had a heart attack. It would have been too nice a death for him, but Micah almost wished for it.

Half of the conclave members turned when they heard him. Elmer looked him up and down, his expression telling Micah what he thought of him. Not that he'd needed that to be aware that Elmer despised him.

"I apologize," he said. He checked his watch. "I thought I was late, but I see I'm not. Did you start the meeting without me?"

Johnson cleared his throat. "Kalliope isn't here yet, either."

Elmer snorted. "Probably because she doesn't know how to check what time it is."

She was famous for being a disaster with technology, including phones and tablets. She was the oldest conclave member, and it showed.

"So there were two of us missing," Micah said as he settled into his chair. He looked around, silently telling the other conclave members what he thought of that behavior.

The meetings always included all the members. That was the point. They decided together what needed to be done about problems and situations, and the members needed to respect those rules.

He wasn't surprised they hadn't.

"We weren't going to make decisions without all of us present," Claire said.

Her blonde hair was neatly tied back in a bun, and she was wearing the heroes' uniform even though she hadn't been one in decades. She was the conclave member who'd always been closest to the heroes, which was why Micah hoped she'd be on his side when the time came. The uniform was severe, but it looked good on her, and he wondered if maybe she'd regretted becoming a conclave member. He didn't have to ask to know that she'd rather have been a hero for the rest of her life, even if it never ended, since she was immortal.

"This is urgent," Verne snapped. "That situation requires attention right now, not when you and Kalliope decide you want to show up."

"If you wanted us to meet sooner, then you should have given us a different time. I was in my office, and I could have been here an hour or two ago." Micah wouldn't let Verne intimidate him. He might be the youngest, but that didn't mean he didn't know what he was doing.

Verne started ranting about the fallen heroes like he had been when Micah came in. Micah kept half of his mind on what Verne was saying, but he allowed his thoughts to wander. He looked at Johnson and Claire. Both of them appeared uncomfortable with what Verne was saying. On the other hand, Elmer and Hester were nodding and clearly approved, which wasn't a surprise. The three had always banded together, and this situation wasn't any different.

Micah wouldn't be able to change their minds, but he hoped something could be done with Johnson and Claire. That would only leave Kalliope, but she was an unknown quantity in this situation, which could be a problem.

She'd never been close to anyone on the conclave, which was a good thing, but it also meant Micah didn't know how she thought. Would she side with Verne and the others, or could she see how problematic the conclave had become?

The volume of Verne's voice rose as Kalliope finally came in.

Micah sighed heavily and settled back in his chair. This was going to be a long meeting, and while he wished he could just leave and let Verne scream himself out, he needed all the information he could get so he could pass it on to Mordred. They had to be aware of what the conclave would decide when it came to the fallen heroes.

Nothing he could do or say would change the mind of Verne, Elmer, and Hester. They'd always considered him too young, even though he'd been a conclave member for several hundred years. He'd tried, but when he'd realized he wouldn't be able to change anything from the inside, he'd decided to try on the outside.

And he'd helped create the fallen heroes.

Constantine laughed at the way Percy wrinkled his nose.

"There's no way I can eat that," Percy said, poking at the food on his plate.

"You should try it. It's tasty."

"It's made of blood." Percy sounded offended and scandalized, as if he'd never eaten blood.

He probably hadn't. He was kind of stuck up, even now that he was part of the fallen heroes, and he'd become a close friend of Constantine.

"I'm sure you'll like it if you try it," Constantine gently pushed.

But Percy was already shaking his head. He pushed his plate away, and Constantine was more than happy to snatch the sausage from it and put it on his own. He cut into it and popped a piece into his mouth, chewing and humming in pleasure.

Yes, eating blood sausages sounded nasty, and he'd rather not think about what was in it as he chewed, but he truly enjoyed the taste.

Percy was still staring at him, horror painting his expression. He didn't seem to be able to look away, not even when Constantine grinned at him.

"What's in that?" Percy asked.

"Blood."

"I know that. I was wondering what else is in it."

"Well, I don't make them myself, and to be honest, I don't want to know what's in it. They're delicious, but it's a bit weird to be eating blood. But I know there are spices like parsley and pepper, and of course, onions. I love onions."

Percy still didn't look convinced, and Constantine didn't blame him. He was trying to open Percy's mind after Percy had spent most of his life with the heroes, but clearly, blood sausage wasn't the best way to do that.

Percy left Constantine to his sausage and instead ate a normal one. He cut it in perfectly equal bites, then ate slowly, entirely focused on the food.

He was an enigma. Percy had been with the conclave for hundreds of years, like most of the heroes, but he wasn't like most of them. He was part siren, which meant he'd had to hide that part of him, because otherwise, the conclave would have killed him. It had taken a while for him to finally see what the conclave was doing and to admit they were in the wrong, which made even less sense, but Constantine was glad that his friend had finally seen the light. It didn't matter how long it had taken him—he was now free of the conclave and had become one of the fallen heroes.

They chatted through the meal. Percy was always a bit stiff when he was with other heroes, almost as if he expected them to reject him. That might have been true once, but he'd become part of their group, and everyone had welcomed him with open arms.

Well, almost everyone. Constantine couldn't ignore the way his friend Bowen was glaring at both of them from his spot down the table. He didn't know what Bowen's problem was, but he wasn't worried. Bowen had always been grumpy, ever since they'd become partners when they both still worked for the conclave. He disliked Percy, which wasn't a surprise, either. He seemed to have forgotten that he'd been a conclave hero once, too, and that if Mordred hadn't given them a chance, they'd probably still be.

Once lunch was over, Constantine headed out. He wanted to swim for a bit in the pool, then maybe train. He hadn't gone far before Bowen found him, though. His friend's expression was thunderous, which made Constantine sigh. Whatever was about to happen, it wouldn't be nice.

"What are you doing?" Bowen demanded to know.

"Headed downstairs to the pool. Why? Do you want to come with me?" They'd been spending less and less time together, mostly because of Bowen's sour disposition. Even though he'd always been grumpy, it had become worse recently, and while Constantine mourned the loss of his friend, he also wouldn't stick around to hear him berate Mordred and what he was doing, especially when it came to Percy.

Bowen glared. "I meant, what are you doing with *him*?"

Him being Percy.

Constantine sighed. "What did you think I was doing? We were eating lunch. You were there, and you saw us."

"You're being friendly."

"What am I supposed to do? Isolate him? He's my friend."

"He shouldn't be," Bowen snapped. "He's a hero."

There they went again. "He's a fallen hero, just like you and me."

"He was a hero until a few weeks ago."

It had been longer than that since Percy had left the conclave, but Constantine doubted Bowen would enjoy the reminder. "So? We've all been where he is. You and I were partners when we worked for the conclave, remember?"

"He's not a real fallen hero. You have to see that. He's biding his time, but I know he still works for the conclave and that he'll strike when we least expect it. I don't want you to get hurt."

Constantine softened. He understood why Bowen couldn't trust Percy. He didn't have that problem himself, but Bowen had always been more hesitant, which wasn't always a bad thing. Bowen was worried, and it made sense that he was trying to warn him away from Percy.

"Look, I know you don't like Percy, but I promise he's a fallen hero now. It would have been easy for him to betray us when he went back to the conclave, but instead, he came home. You have to let go of the anger you harbor against him."

"He's gotten to you," Bowen whispered.

Constantine almost rolled his eyes. "Is that what you think? What do you think he did to Bay, then?" Those two were together and clearly in love.

"I don't know what he did to him, but I wouldn't be surprised if he used his siren ability against Bay." Bowen paused. "And maybe against you, too."

Constantine had enough. "Percy is my friend, and he's not doing anything to me or anyone else. I understand why you're wary of him, but this has to stop. You don't have to be friendly to him, or even welcoming, but stop trying to undermine our friendship. Unlike you, I trust Percy, and he won't hurt me or any other fallen hero. He's on our side, and he's working with us, and I don't know why you can't accept that and move on."

"I'm worried about you."

"I realize that, but I don't want you to be. Percy won't hurt me." Constantine was sure of that.

It didn't matter that Percy had worked for the conclave a few months ago. Like Constantine had told Bowen, they'd all been in Percy's position once, and more heroes would be when the time came. They were finally realizing that the conclave had changed, and not for the better, which meant that more heroes would leave and join the fight against the conclave.

Percy was one of those heroes. His situation was different because the fallen heroes had captured him, and at the time, he'd trusted the conclave and had wanted to go back, but he'd seen the light. Percy wasn't going anywhere, especially not when Bay was one of the leaders of the fallen heroes. He and Bay were together, and that was never going to change. Constantine didn't have to ask them to be certain of that. They loved each other in a way that made him yearn for something

9

he hadn't had in a long time, if ever.

"Percy won't hurt me," he repeated. "And even though you and I were friends for a long time, I don't think we can be any longer if you can't accept my friendship with him."

Bowen jerked back. "You're choosing him over me?"

"Are you asking me to choose?"

Because if he was, they both knew who Constantine would pick, and it wouldn't be Bowen.

CHAPTER TWO

Something was about to happen. Micah didn't know what, but the other conclave members wouldn't just hang back and wait for the fallen heroes to make their next move. They were planning something, but there was no trust between them, even though they all belonged to the conclave. They wouldn't tell Micah anything, and that made him nervous.

He'd been nervous since the meeting a few days ago. Verne, Elmer, and Hester were their own little group within the conclave, intent on keeping everything as it was. They never listened when Micah suggested changes, and they were usually the ones who gave the worst orders when it came to dealing with supernatural creatures. They wanted all of them to die, no matter what kind of person they were, which was one of the things Micah was trying to change.

So he wasn't surprised when his personal assistant slammed into his office without knocking on the door. Daniel's eyes were wide, and he was pale as if he'd seen a ghost.

Micah shot to his feet, almost toppling his chair on the floor. "What is it?"

"They're arresting Marsha."

Micah swore. He should have expected it. The conclave had no proof, but they suspected that Marsha had helped Haven escape after he'd been arrested. Micah had been more than happy to close an eye, but obviously, the rest of the conclave hadn't. Still, they should have voted on this, considering who Marsha was. She was one of the most experienced heroes, and while she'd mainly stopped going on missions, she was a handler and a trainer. She was vital to the conclave's mission, or at least to what the conclave's mission should be.

And now, she was being arrested. If things went the way they usually did, she'd also be tortured, then put on trial. If the conclave found a majority, she'd be put to death. Micah was only one person. Even if he voted against it, it might only be his vote against six others, and it wouldn't be enough.

He had to do something before things came to that.

He ran out of the office, Daniel right behind him. He had to let Daniel take the lead, and he wasn't surprised when his assistant headed toward Marsha's office. He also wasn't surprised to find a small crowd gathered there, watching what was happening.

Micah pushed into the crowd, thankful for his conclave position, because it meant the heroes let him pass once they realized who he was. When he got to the front, he found Hester, Elmer, and Verne standing in a little group, all of them looking satisfied. Marsha was in front of them, her hands behind her back, a hero putting handcuffs on her. She looked calm and unworried, so she'd probably expected something like this to happen, just like Micah had.

That didn't mean it should be happening.

"What's going on?" Micah asked as he strode forward.

Hester, Verne, and Elmer all glared at him. "We're arresting a traitor," Verne said.

Micah crossed his arms over his chest. He wasn't intimidated by Verne or by how many more years he'd been a conclave member. "This wasn't discussed in the last meeting we had."

"It didn't need to be discussed. She's a traitor, and she has to pay."

"You can't arrest a hero, especially one so important to our mission, without bringing it up at the meeting and voting on it."

Verne's smile was gleeful. "We did vote on it. We had a majority, and we're arresting her."

Micah did his best not to look surprised. He looked around, finally finding Claire. She was standing behind the group of three, looking as if she'd rather be anywhere but there. Micah was sad that she'd voted with the other three but not surprised.

He turned his attention back to Vern. "How could this be a legitimate vote when the entire conclave wasn't made aware of what was happening? You didn't ask *me* to vote on this."

Vern waved Micah's words away. "We didn't need to. We had a majority, and we did what we had to." He looked at the hero who'd been handcuffing Marsha. "You. Take her to the cells."

Another hero stepped up, and together, they framed Marsha. She started walking without them having to threaten her. They walked toward Micah, and he stepped in their path, ready to stop them.

"We're just following orders," one of the heroes said. He didn't look at Micah or anyone else, but he appeared defeated.

Micah glanced around. Of all the heroes present at the arrest, only a couple looked like they agreed with what was happening. Most of them respected Marsha and even liked her, and they didn't want her to die. The hero was right. He was following orders, and there was no way for Micah to go against the conclave, not when they had a majority of votes. He'd have to find another way to save Marsha. It wouldn't help to get this hero or any other in trouble with the rest of the conclave. If anything, it would make things worse, and that wasn't what Micah was trying to do.

He sucked in a breath and stepped to the side. He nodded at the heroes, then turned his attention to Marsha. "I'll get you out of there," he promised.

"Don't get in trouble because of me," she whispered as she

walked by.

Micah watched her walk down the hallway, already thinking about a way to get her out. He turned to head to his office once she was out of sight, but Verne stepped forward to confront him.

"Who are you working for?" Verne asked.

Micah arched a brow. "Humanity, just like you."

"You know very well that's not what I was talking about. You're not working for the heroes. You're not working with the conclave."

"Are you insinuating something?"

Verne got in Micah's face. "Damn right I am. If you were truly a conclave member, you'd work with us, not against us. Instead, you wanted to free the traitor."

"We don't have any proof she's a traitor."

"We don't need proof," Verne yelled. "She helped that hero escape, and that's enough for me."

"You don't know that she helped him. If I remember right, there were reports that supernatural creatures were involved."

"I don't care. That hero was her responsibility, and he escaped. She'll pay for that."

Nothing Micah could say would change Verne's mind, so he didn't try. His heart raced as he turned around, ignoring Verne's yells for him to come back. He had nothing to say to Verne or Elmer and Hester. He'd have liked to ask Claire why she went along with this, but he didn't want to yell at her like Verne was yelling at him. He was tempted to do that and take his anger out on her. It wouldn't help get her to his side, which was what he needed.

So instead, he went back to his office. Daniel trailed behind him, silent and clearly worried. He was one of the younger heroes, and he hadn't been on many missions. He was still learning how to fight and deal with supernatural creatures, which was why he worked for Micah in the meantime. Micah liked him, and he could tell that his heart wasn't into fighting but that he enjoyed his job. He hoped he'd be able to help Daniel and all the other heroes who wanted nothing to do with the fights—they just wanted to find a life they truly wanted to live.

But that would only come once the conclave was dealt with, and they weren't there yet.

"I don't want to see anyone," Micah said once they reached the office.

Daniel nodded. "I'll keep them away."

"But don't get in trouble. If one of the three demands to see me, let them in. Just tell me first, all right?"

Micah locked the door to his office. He waited for a moment, breathing in and out as he tried to calm himself. Once he wasn't freaking out anymore, he strode to his desk.

He didn't use the phone provided to all conclave members. That wouldn't have been smart. Instead, he dipped his hand into the vase on the corner of his desk. Daniel kept it supplied with fresh flowers, and while they looked nice, that wasn't why Micah wanted it to be on his desk.

His fingers touched something hard, and he pulled it out. He made sure not to get anything wet as he opened the plastic cover and discarded it. Once he had his phone in his hand, he quickly dialed a number he knew by heart.

"I didn't expect to hear from you so soon after the last time you called," Mordred drawled when he answered.

Micah couldn't help but smile at the sound of his friend's voice.

He and Mordred had worked together a long time ago. They'd been heroes at the same time, and while they hadn't been in the same team, they'd become close, even though they weren't supposed to be. Heroes weren't here to make friends. They were here to help humanity, and that was what they had to focus on.

When Mordred had left, Micah had been tempted to do the same. It would have been easier for him than sticking around, but he'd wanted to change things, and he'd believed he could do it as a conclave member. He should have known better, and he supposed he did now, but he hadn't given up. If there was anything he could do to change what was happening, he would.

"We have a problem," he said.

Constantine had his face pressed against the mat when he heard his cell phone ring. He rolled onto his back, grinned up at Percy, and got to his feet. "Looks like someone's calling me."

Percy crossed his arms over his chest and glared. "You're only trying to get out of training."

"I'm trying to get out of getting my ass kicked."

"You'll never get better if you don't even try."

"I *was* trying. It's not my fault you're much better than I am."

And Percy was. Constantine was great with weapons, especially guns, which was a recent development for heroes. He'd never touched one while he was still with the conclave, but Mordred had introduced him to them, and while they wouldn't kill a hero, they did enough damage to be useful.

He wiped the sweat off his face and headed toward the bench, relieved for the interruption. He had to keep up with his training, but he didn't particularly enjoy getting his ass kicked by Percy.

His phone had stopped ringing, but it started again right after he found it. It was Mordred, which probably meant Constantine was about to be sent on a mission. Either that or he was in trouble, but he couldn't think of anything he might have done recently.

"Mordred?" he asked when he answered.

"I need you to come to my office."

"I'll be right there. Has something happened?"

"In a way. I'll tell you when you get here."

"Do I have time to go shower?"

"Only if you're quick."

It was the fastest shower he'd ever taken. His hair was still wet as he walked down the hallways toward Mordred's office. He wasn't surprised to see he wasn't the only one there when he arrived. Haven was present, too, along with Bay and Mordred, and they all looked worried.

"Sorry I'm late," Constantine said as he closed the door. "I was training."

Mordred pointed at the only empty chair on the other side of his desk, and Constantine took a seat.

"My contact in the conclave just called me," he explained. "Marsha, Haven's old handler, has been arrested. There are plans to torture her, then put her on trial and eventually execute her."

Constantine swore and leaned back in his chair. He remembered Marsha, even though she hadn't been his handler. Haven looked like someone had kicked him in the nuts, though. "We have to help her," he said.

Mordred nodded. "I agree. Even if she doesn't want to become a fallen hero, she needs to be saved before she's killed."

"And you're sure this is happening?" Bay asked.

"Micah just called me to let me know."

Constantine had been shocked to find out that one of the conclave members was helping the fallen heroes. Apparently, Micah disliked what the conclave had become, and Constantine couldn't disagree. He remembered Micah, but they'd never had much contact. The conclave stayed separate from the heroes unless they put one on trial, which was never a good thing. But Micah was a good person—and a gorgeous one. His gray eyes had fascinated Constantine, and he was glad Micah was one of the good guys.

"He's in danger?" Haven asked.

Mordred sighed. "He won't tell me, but I think we all know the answer to that. Hester, Verne, and Elmer got the majority when they convinced Claire to vote with them. Micah suspects they forced her somehow, but there's no way to know for sure. He also said that Verne asked him who he was working for. That means that at least he suspects something's going on with Micah, which I don't like."

"He needs to leave."

"I wish it was easy to convince him of that, but so far, he's brushed me off every time I suggested it." Mordred looked at Constantine. "I want you to be ready to extract Marsha as soon as I have news from Micah."

"I will be."

"You're not going alone. You usually work with Bowen, so he'll be going with you."

Constantine hesitated. He didn't want to talk badly about Bowen, but he didn't think this was a good idea considering the last few interactions they'd had. "I think it would be better if you sent someone else with me."

Mordred looked surprised. "Is there something wrong?"

"I don't know. Bowen has been behaving strangely since Percy arrived. He's angry that I became Percy's friend, and he made sure I knew it. There's a lot of anger in him, and I don't think that sending him to the conclave will help."

Mordred stared for a moment before nodding. "You know him better than I do, so we'll go along with what you think is best. Pick someone else then, and let them know what's happening. I trust you to choose someone who won't tell anyone about the situation. Only a few selected people know about Micah, and it has to stay that way. We can't afford for him to be in danger because someone can't keep their mouth shut."

It would probably be easier to choose someone who already knew about Micah. "Haven could go with me," he suggested.

"I'd be happy to," Haven said.

"We could also take Thor. Having a creature with us could give us an advantage that heroes won't have."

"Why Thor and not Tryg?" Mordred asked. The corner of his lips twitched, telling Constantine he knew the reason behind it.

"Because everyone's scared of him. The guy will tear your head off just for looking at his man. I tried talking to Isaac the other day, and I swear Tryg growled at me."

Mordred laughed. "Thor it is, then. The three of you need to be ready, so I'll let him know about this. For now, we stay back and wait. Micah is going to try to get Marsha out without having to bring us in, but I doubt that's going to work."

"Are we still going to that meeting this afternoon?" Constantine was excited that Mordred had chosen him to talk to the heroes who were leaving the conclave. They couldn't accept all of them in the fallen heroes, and they certainly couldn't welcome them in the home they shared without knowing whether or not they were trustworthy. That meant they had to talk to every hero, find out what they wanted to do and what they were ready to do, and decide whether or not they should work together. Usually, the decision was yes, because they needed as many people as possible to defeat the conclave.

With so many heroes questioning what the conclave was doing and reaching out to the fallen heroes, they needed more people to talk to them and find out what to do next. Constantine had volunteered, but he hadn't thought Mordred would choose him. But he had, and Constantine enjoyed this part of the work.

Mordred nodded. "It's important we go. I doubt Micah will manage to do anything that quickly. Since he wants to talk to the other conclave members, it's going to take him a while, so we'll have time to go."

"How many emails are still coming in?" Haven asked.

"Too many for us to be able to deal with this easily. But it's a good thing. It means many people understand that what the conclave is doing is wrong and that they're ready to fight. They just want some reassurance first, and that's what we're giving them."

"I hope it will be enough to defeat the conclave," Haven murmured.

They all looked at each other. Constantine felt the same, and he was sure that Bay and Mordred did, too.

The conclave was a formidable enemy, but it was an enemy they had to deal with. They couldn't ignore what was happening or the fact that unless someone stepped in, it would continue happening until there was not even one supernatural creature left on earth.

Constantine couldn't allow that. Some of his friends were supernatural creatures, and he loved them. So he was going to fight the conclave, and he'd make sure the fallen heroes won.

He wouldn't even consider a different outcome.

Micah didn't have much time left, which meant he had to do everything he could before he was run out of the conclave. His first instinct was to stay as far away from the other conclave members as he could, but he couldn't risk it. The only way to deal with the conclave would be to kill all the members, which wouldn't start the new order the way he wanted, or to try to convince the majority to side with him to get rid of the worst members.

He would never convince Verne, Elmer, and Hester. He wouldn't even try, because it wouldn't be safe for him. If he tried talking about changes, their first reaction would be to have him arrested, and he had no intention to let that happen.

But he might be able to convince Johnson and Claire, which would put him and Verne at an equal number of conclave members. Kalliope would be the one to make the final decision, and while Micah had no idea which way she would go, it wouldn't stop him from contacting her.

First, the ones he was sure he could convince.

He wouldn't tell them about what he was doing with the fallen heroes just yet. He couldn't afford to, but he could try to get Marsha freed. Surely they had to see what was happening. Claire especially was Micah's target. He didn't know why she'd voted with the other three to have Marsha arrested, but he suspected she'd been forced somehow, and he wanted that to change. If it couldn't, well, he had Mordred on speed dial, and the man was waiting for a call from him. He and his people would take care of Marsha, and hopefully, no one would get hurt as they did so.

Micah hesitated. He didn't want to leave his office in case he saw one of the other conclave members, but a phone call didn't feel like enough. Maybe a video call? He wouldn't be able to get Kalliope that way, but she could wait, at least for now.

He woke up his computer and quickly clicked around. Usually, he had Daniel organize this kind of meeting, but he didn't want to pull his personal assistant in. If anything happened, Verne and the others would try to get Daniel arrested, too, and Micah didn't want him to get hurt. It was better if he kept all of this away from him so he could say he hadn't known anything.

Micah decided to call Johnson and Claire at the same time. He hoped they'd both answer, because they didn't have time to waste.

Johnson answered right away. He blinked at Micah, a frown on his face. "What's going on?"

Micah leaned back in his chair. "Do you know about Marsha?"

Johnson's expression shifted. "I do. We weren't consulted."

"We weren't," Micah agreed. "When I pointed that out, Verne said he didn't need to consult us because he already had the majority of votes."

"Who?"

Johnson and Claire were somewhat close. Johnson wouldn't have been surprised if Kalliope had been the fourth vote, but the heartbreak in his expression when Micah told him it had been Claire made Micah wonder if there was more than friendship between them. It was none of his business, but the other conclave members would pitch a fit if they found out.

"I don't know why she did this," Johnson said.

Micah's gaze flicked to the other side of the screen because Claire had finally answered. "We're about to find out," he said. "Claire. Johnson is on this video call, too."

She was in her office. She was still wearing the uniform, but she looked distraught. "You're calling about Marsha," she said.

"Why did you vote for her arrest?"

"Because I had to."

"Did they force you?" It was dangerous to say that out loud. Not one of the conclave members trusted the others, but it was still a sign of disrespect, and more importantly, it could be dangerous.

Claire hesitated, then shook her head. "Verne came to me and explained why he thought Marsha should be arrested. He's not wrong. She didn't try to stop that hero from getting away."

"There were supernatural creatures involved."

"And she should have fought them. She's a handler, and she was a fighter before. Her hero had been condemned to death, and she should have honored that."

Something was happening with Claire. Micah tried to read her expression, but it was closed off. She didn't want him to find out what was going on, and unless he stuck his nose around, he wouldn't.

"We need to get organized so she won't be condemned to death," he said. "If the three of us vote against it and I manage to convince Kalliope to do the same, we'll have the majority."

But Claire was already shaking her head. "I'm sorry. I already told Verne I'd vote with him on this."

"Claire, please. You know Marsha doesn't deserve to die. Don't let Verne push you into something you'll regret."

"She's a traitor, and she has to pay. I'm sorry, Micah." She hesitated. "But you should be careful. You won't like what will happen if Verne finds out about this call."

She hung up before Micah could say anything else. He stared at her side of the screen for a second, knowing something had happened but unable to understand what. Then, he looked at Johnson. "Do you know what Verne did to her?"

Johnson shook his head. "I have no idea, but I don't like it."

"I don't, either. You think you could convince her?"

"Normally, I'd say yes, but I'm not sure. I'll try to call her, or maybe go see her, but I'm not making any promises. You do have to be careful, though, Micah. Claire is right. Verne and the other two won't be happy if they find out you're working against them."

Micah wanted to scream. He was working against the conclave much more than Johnson and Claire could imagine. He'd be put to death if they found out, but that wouldn't be enough to get him to back down. He was convinced that what he was doing was the only thing he could do in this situation, and he wouldn't stop.

But he wouldn't get Marsha out of her cell this way, which meant he had to find another option. He'd have to contact Mordred, but first he wanted to check in on Marsha. It probably wasn't the smartest thing to do because it would put a target on his back, but he wasn't abandoning her. She'd done the right thing, letting Haven go, and no one would ever convince Micah of the opposite.

His video meeting hadn't yielded the result he'd hoped, but it didn't stop him from leaving his office once it was over. He headed toward the cells, hoping Marsha hadn't been tortured yet but knowing that even if she hadn't, it wouldn't be long. Verne would want her trial to be organized as soon as possible, which meant he wouldn't have a lot of time to get whatever answers he thought he could get out of her.

He crossed paths with a few heroes on the way there, but no one tried to stop him until he reached the cells. There, the two heroes who'd taken Marsha to her cell stepped forward, but they knew better than to order him not to do anything.

"Verne ordered not to let anyone talk to her," the one who hadn't spoken to Micah before said.

Micah tried to remember the names of all the heroes he worked with, but there had been so many of them over the decades that sometimes, it wasn't possible.

He straightened his back, trying to make himself look taller. He didn't really need it to be imposing since he was a conclave member and six foot two, but still. He'd take every bit of help he could get in this situation.

"The last time I checked, I had the same kind of authority as Verne. He's a conclave member, as am I. Why do his orders have more weight than mine?"

"They don't," the hero said, looking everywhere but at Micah. "But he had the majority."

"Which is why I couldn't stop him from arresting Marsha.

I doubt he put the fact that no one could visit her to a vote, though." Micah didn't want these heroes to get in trouble, and he understood why they were trying to stop him. "Look, I just want to make sure she's okay. I won't tell Verne or anyone else about this visit, and as long as you don't either, no one will find out."

"There are cameras, sir," the other hero stepped in.

"I'll make sure Verne doesn't find out." Some conclave members disliked technology and didn't think they should learn it, but Micah disagreed.

He could use a computer easily, and he'd made sure to learn as many skills as he could over the years. He was pretty sure he could get into the computers and destroy the video of him talking to Marsha, and if he couldn't, he'd contact Mordred and ask his people to do it. Either way, no one would find out he'd visited Marsha, and he hoped these two heroes would believe it.

They looked at each other, then the first one finally nodded. "You can talk to her, but you have to be fast."

"I will be." It wasn't like they had much to say to each other anyway.

Micah just wanted to make sure she was okay and to reassure her that he was working on getting her out. The problem was that he didn't know how long it would take, which meant Marsha would no doubt be tortured in the meantime.

But as soon as he was back in his office, he'd be calling Mordred and asking him to get Marsha out.

Mordred was visibly still worried when he and Constantine left the house. Constantine wanted to reassure him, but he doubted he could. They both knew Micah was in danger and would be until he left the conclave, and it was obvious he didn't want to.

Constantine admired him for wanting to change things and for attempting to do so from the inside, but he didn't think it would work. The only thing it would do was put Micah in danger, and he hoped nothing would happen to the man. It wasn't just because they needed him for information, either. Micah was trying to do the right thing like everyone else should be, and it wouldn't be fair for only him to pay for that.

"Can you remind me of the names of the heroes we're about to meet?" he asked Mordred. He needed to distract himself so he wouldn't obsess over what might be happening to Micah and Marsha right now.

Mordred arched a brow. "You didn't read the email I sent you?"

"I might have been busy."

Thankfully, Mordred didn't look angry. He just rolled his eyes and turned his attention back to where he was walking.

They were headed away from the house, deeper into the forest, where they'd open a portal. There was no way they'd meet any of the heroes leaving the conclave at the house. It was their safe place and home to several supernatural creatures. They couldn't afford to bring heroes they weren't sure they could trust here.

"The email I got was from a hero named Benson. From what he said, he's a recent hero."

"Which is probably why he's more ready than others to listen to us."

Mordred nodded. "No doubt. He mentioned two of his friends wanted to see me, too. Petra and Juliet. I had the feeling that there might be something between him and Juliet, but I couldn't say for sure. As for Petra, well, she's his partner."

"I'm surprised the conclave still uses partners."

One of the rules the conclave had created was that heroes couldn't fraternize. They couldn't be together, and they shouldn't be friends. That was one of the reasons they'd stopped partnering heroes eventually, but for thousands of years, heroes had gone out in pairs. It had been safer, and it would still be, but the conclave didn't like heroes being close to people, not even other heroes. As far as Constantine knew, he and Bowen had been some of the last to be partnered. He was pretty sure they would have been split up if they'd stayed with the conclave, and he was glad they hadn't. Although considering Bowen's recent behavior, maybe it wouldn't have been a problem.

Mordred shrugged. "It might be because Benson is such a recent hero." He stopped in the middle of the forest and raised a hand. Constantine had always been in awe about how easily Mordred created portals. He knew it was all because of practice, and he could create portals, too, but not the way Mordred did.

Once the portal was open, Mordred gestured at Constantine to step in. Constantine was ready for a fight, but he shouldn't have worried. While the place they landed in was empty of people, Constantine could hear the sound of humans walking and talking close by.

He quickly looked around. The building was empty, both of people and furniture. He wasn't sure it was abandoned, because it looked in decent shape, but even if it wasn't, no one would walk in on them talking. There was a window close by, and when he peeked through it, he noticed they were above a busy street.

It was wise of Benson to choose this place for their talk. He knew Mordred and Constantine wouldn't try anything with so many humans around. It was essential to eliminate the conclave, but it was just as important to make sure humans never found out about the supernatural world.

Mordred appeared next to Constantine, and the portal vanished. He looked around, nodded, and turned his attention to Constantine. "Do you remember any of the three I mentioned?"

Constantine had to think back. "Maybe Juliet? I mean, her name isn't uncommon, so it might not be the same person I'm thinking about."

"I take it the two of you weren't close."

"I was never close to anyone except Bowen."

"Pity, but I understand."

It hadn't been safe for Constantine to be close to anyone when the conclave explicitly forbid it.

They both heard footsteps coming closer at the same time, and they turned as one in that direction. The young man appeared, looking wary, and Constantine knew they were in front of Benson.

He wore the hero uniform, which would make sense if he hadn't left the conclave yet. Benson's gaze went from Constantine to Mordred, stopping there. Benson looked impressed but also a bit scared.

"I'm Constantine," Constantine said, stepping forward but keeping his distance. "You must be Benson."

Benson nodded. "Thank you for coming." His voice was smooth and a delight to listen to.

"I think you mentioned another two heroes?"

Benson hesitated, then waved a hand over his shoulder. Seconds later, two women appeared.

Juliet was the hero Constantine remembered. He waved at her, and her eyes widened, maybe because she recognized him.

"Hello, Juliet," he said.

"The two of you know each other?" Benson asked.

The other woman, Petra, snorted. "Most heroes know each other, at least by sight. Constantine hasn't been with the conclave for a while, though."

"I left a few decades ago," he explained to Benson. "When I did, I was in the same place you are in now, although it was more complicated, since I didn't know about the fallen heroes. I had no one to ask my questions to and no answers. What I did was a step of faith, and I'm glad I did it."

"We just want to talk," Juliet said.

Constantine smiled. "Then let's talk. Mordred and I will answer any questions you have as long as we know the answers."

This was a job Constantine was made for. As one of the more recent fallen heroes, he understood well where these three were coming from. He supposed Mordred could have sent Percy instead, but Percy was prickly on his best days and a nightmare to deal with on the worst. He'd probably tell them to either leave the conclave or fuck off, which wasn't the best way to get them to join the fallen heroes in their fight.

"Why did you leave the conclave?" Juliet asked.

"There were several reasons, but the main one was that they sent my partner and me on a mission. We were supposed to kill a nest of harpies that had been terrorizing humans. Or at least that's what we were told. When we got there, we realized that most of the harpies were too young to do what the conclave said they were doing. Some were barely more than babies. It was a group of mothers and children, and there was no way Bowen and I were going to kill them. We were sure the conclave had made a mistake, although I had some doubts considering some of the things we heard from other heroes. We contacted our handler, and he ordered us to do what we were told. One of the conclave members confirmed the mission. We had to kill the harpies, and it didn't matter how young they were."

Constantine remembered that day well, and he was glad he'd left. He never wanted to find himself in that situation again. The poor harpies had been terrified, and even though he'd done everything he could to reassure them, he'd still been a hero, and heroes killed harpies.

"Bowen and I talked about it, and we agreed we couldn't do it. We helped the harpies escape and find a safer place to stay. Then, we just never went back to the conclave. We heard about some of the heroes leaving the conclave and banding together, and we decided it would be safer for us to be with them. It took us a little while to find Mordred, but when we did, he welcomed us, and we've been working with him since then."

"Do we have to work with the fallen heroes if we decide to leave the conclave?" Petra asked.

"You'll be allowed to do whatever you want," Mordred intervened. "That's another thing we disagree with. The conclave wants full control over heroes, and it's unfair. We might be heroes, but we're also human beings with feelings, needs, and wants. If you never want to fight again, we'll help you find a new home and be safe, and you'll be able to do whatever you want with your life."

It was time to let Mordred speak now, so Constantine took a step back. He hoped they'd be able to convince these three to come to their side, but he understood how hard it was. Fighting other heroes to get rid of the conclave would be like fighting family, and unfortunately, it was something they'd have to do soon.

CHAPTER THREE

When Daniel ran into Micah's office, Micah knew something terrible had happened. For a moment, he thought Marsha had been executed. He wouldn't be surprised if Verne and the others went behind his back and did it without telling him. Verne would probably want to do it with as much drama as possible so every hero knew what awaited them if they betrayed the conclave, but he knew Micah would be against that. It would be easier to do it swiftly, and Micah fully expected Daniel to tell him that was what happened.

"Verne went to the cells," Daniel said, out of breath. "He's torturing Marsha."

Micah swore. He supposed it was better than executing her, but not by much. The conclave members were old and knew every single way to torture someone. If they wanted Marsha to be in pain for days, she would be. Hester probably wouldn't get her hands dirty, but Micah wouldn't put it past Verne and Elmer.

He ran out the door, knowing he'd only have this chance to stop it. It probably wouldn't be for long, either, which meant that as soon as he could, he'd have to call Mordred and tell him to send someone to get Marsha. She couldn't stay, not when she was in this much danger.

Having her disappear would complicate Micah's life and his plans, but he could deal with it if it meant she was safe. It wasn't like he had a choice.

He could hear Daniel running beside him, but he didn't look at him. His entire focus was on getting to the cells, and even if he hadn't known where they were, he'd have found out because of the screams. He followed them, surprised when he realized Marsha wasn't the one screaming, but rather, a hero in the cell next to hers, who was trying to get Verne to stop hurting her.

Micah marched into the cell where Marsha had been placed.

She was sitting in a chair at the center of the room. Two heroes stood behind her, one of them holding her in place. Her blonde hair was messy and plastered to the side of her face with blood. Verne stood in front of her, the wounds on his knuckles telling Micah what he'd been doing.

When Marsha straightened, Micah saw that her lip was bleeding, and her cheek was quickly swelling. One of her eyes had a cut at the corner, and if he had to bet, he'd say she'd have a black eye in a few hours.

"What's going on?" he demanded to know, putting all his authority into his voice. He was lucky that only Verne was here. He was the most dangerous of the bunch, but he tended to stay back when his two friends didn't support him.

"What are you doing here? This is none of your business," Verne snapped.

Micah tried to appear calm. "None of my business? The last time I checked, I was a conclave member with the same authority to make this kind of decision and be included as you. Why are you the only one here? Did you have a majority to torture Marsha, or are you doing this on your own?"

Micah knew he had Verne when Verne's gaze skittered away from him. It didn't last long, but it was enough, and he felt better. He'd be able to buy more time for Marsha. Verne hadn't told anyone about this, which meant they hadn't voted on torturing Marsha. He was doing this entirely on his own, which was forbidden.

"What did you think would happen when she was

arrested?" Verne asked.

"That we'd talk about this and vote before you decided to torture her. Step back from her."

Verne's hands tightened into fists. He obeyed, moving away from Marsha, but it meant he moved toward Micah.

Micah was ready. He might be younger than Verne, but it didn't mean he was useless. Besides, Verne and his friends didn't train with the heroes anymore. They thought they didn't need to, and they'd become complacent. If they had to fight, Micah thought he had a good chance of winning, and he hedged to get his hands on Verne.

"How dare you?" Verne said with a growl.

"You and I are equal," Micah said. "Just like the other conclave members are equal to us. You have no right to do this on your own without talking to us first. Don't think I forgot how you got the votes to arrest her in the first place. You should have called a meeting, but you went behind our backs, which means you know that what you're doing is wrong. If you want to execute Marsha, fine. Call for a meeting, and let's vote."

Verne obviously wanted to protest, but he couldn't. They weren't alone, and the heroes present in the room were listening. Even though heroes weren't supposed to fraternize, Micah had no doubt that in half an hour, every single hero still working for the conclave would know what had just happened. They'd know that Verne had tried going behind the conclave's back and killing someone most of them cared about and that Micah had stepped in.

Micah wouldn't allow anyone else to hurt Marsha, which meant he'd have to get her out of here. He was a traitor, but he didn't care because it was the right thing to do.

Verne looked at the other heroes and huffed. "Fine. You'll have your meeting. But you know I have the majority on this."

"Maybe, maybe not. I suppose we'll see when we vote."

Verne twirled around and stomped out. Micah watched him go, just in case Verne decided to change his mind and come back. When he didn't, Micah relaxed. He turned to look at Marsha, who was staring at him from her chair. Her eye was swelling, and Micah knew all too well the state she'd be in a few hours.

"Get some ice for her eye," he ordered the heroes.

They didn't hesitate. They ran out of the room, which Micah hoped meant they disagreed with what Verne had been doing. Since they had a few minutes on their own, he crouched next to Marsha and gently touched her arm. "How are you?"

She chuckled, then winced. "Don't say stupid things and make me laugh. How do you think I am?"

"It *was* a stupid question," Micah agreed. "I never wanted anything like this to happen to you."

"I knew it was a possibility when I helped Haven escape."

"So you did do it?"

"It's more like I looked the other way, but the conclave probably won't see it the way I do."

She was right, unfortunately. "I'll get you out of here."

Marsha's good eye narrowed. "What are you planning?"

"I don't want you to worry about it."

"How can I not? I can see you're going to get yourself in trouble."

Micah grinned. "Isn't that why I'm a conclave member? You deserve none of this. I won't stand by and watch as Verne tortures and kills you."

"But he's right. I did betray the conclave."

"You betrayed this conclave, but you wouldn't have if the conclave had been balanced and making good decisions."

She sucked in a breath. "If Verne hears you . . ."

"He won't. Hang on for a few more hours."

She opened her mouth, but before she could ask what was

on her mind, the two heroes came back. Micah got to his feet and left without looking at Marsha again. He had work to do, and the sooner he did it, the better it would be for her.

Daniel was waiting outside the block of cells. He was pale and looked like he'd rather be anywhere but here, which was becoming a theme when it came to Micah's personal assistant.

"How is she?" he asked when he saw Micah.

"You got to me in time. I stopped Verne from doing anything too bad."

Daniel's shoulders slumped. "Thank god."

"Keep an eye on what's happening here, will you? I have something to do."

Daniel stared at Micah for a moment before nodding. "Will you be doing anything that puts you in danger?"

Even though Daniel hadn't been working for Micah for long, he already knew him too well. "Don't worry about me."

"How can I not? You're one of the few good ones here." He looked around, then leaned closer. "If I can help you, I will."

It touched Micah, but he didn't want to get Daniel in trouble. This was Micah's problem, and he'd deal with it on his own, or rather, with the help of the fallen heroes.

Constantine wasn't surprised when he got the call from Mordred that he, Haven, and Thor had to pick up Marsha. He'd expected it to happen sooner rather than later, and he was relieved they'd be able to help. Hopefully, they'd get there before she was tortured, but he remembered well how the conclave worked.

He wasn't sure what to expect. He hadn't been at the conclave building since he'd left the heroes, and he hadn't believed he'd go back until the final fight. He didn't know what he'd find, but from the outside, everything looked the way it had when he'd still worked for the conclave.

They'd arrived by portal, but they couldn't sneak into the building that way.

"Ready?" Thor asked.

He was smiling, almost as if he was enjoying himself. Constantine suspected he was. Thor wanted the conclave to pay for what they'd done over the years, and he liked fighting. This situation combined the two in the best of ways.

Haven and Constantine looked at each other and nodded. When Thor offered them his hands, they each took one. Constantine had never become smoke with one of the draugr who worked with the fallen heroes, and he was excited. He held his breath, but he didn't feel like anything happened, at least until he looked down at himself. Then, he found himself grinning like a loon.

Could he even grin since he was smoke?

Are the two of you okay? Thor's voice asked in Constantine's mind. It made sense that they couldn't speak, since they didn't have a mouth at the moment.

I hate this, Haven's grumpy voice answered.

Constantine? Everything okay? Thor continued.

I'm perfect, Constantine said.

He heard Thor chuckle in his mind. *Great. We're moving in.*

They stopped talking after that, and Constantine focused on what they were about to do. Thor seemed to know where he was going. He entered from under the front door, then moved them down hallways. He paused a few times, and Haven was the one to give him directions when he needed them.

They'd thought to go directly to the cells, but it had been deemed too dangerous. If some of the heroes guarding the cells realized that they were there, they'd be in trouble, and that wasn't something they wanted to deal with. So instead of heading toward the cells, they went to Micah's office.

Constantine had been surprised when Mordred had told him that was where they needed to go. Micah worked with them, but could he put himself in so much danger? They were here to pick up Marsha, and if she was in Micah's office, it meant he'd gotten her out of the cell and to the office with no one noticing.

Or maybe someone *had* noticed, and right now, they were headed to Micah's office, too.

They had to be fast. Thankfully, smoke moved quickly, and after a few minutes, they slid under yet another door. Thor stopped them in the middle of the room, and Constantine quickly looked around. They were in an office, just like they were supposed to be. Marsha was sitting on a chair in front of the desk, holding something against her eye. Micah stood next to her, talking, but he looked around as if he could feel something was wrong. Constantine wondered if Mordred had explained how they would rescue Marsha. He wasn't even sure Micah knew the fallen heroes worked with supernatural creatures.

Constantine and the other two suddenly were solid again. Constantine stumbled, but it was easy enough to get his bearings. Micah twirled around, half crouching in a defensive position, at least until he recognized Haven.

"You're here for Marsha?" he asked.

Haven nodded. "We're taking her away." He took a step toward her, then stopped. "How are you?" he asked her.

She lowered the thing she'd been holding against her eye. Someone had beaten her up, and half of her face was turning black and blue. Constantine had seen much worse when he'd been with the heroes, but he was still angry. She hadn't deserved this. She might have looked the other way when Haven had been rescued, but it was the right thing to do, and the conclave members knew that. They might not like it, but they had to be aware of what a disaster they were. Instead of protecting the people they were supposed to protect, they were killing them, all so they could keep their power and authority.

"Do all men ask stupid questions?" Marsha asked.

Haven blinked, and Constantine found himself snickering. When he looked up, he noticed that Micah was staring at him. He smiled, not knowing what to think of the conclave member.

Constantine should hate him, but Micah was doing what he could to keep the conclave under control and to fight them from the inside, and Constantine thought that was sneaky. It also was necessary. They couldn't take the conclave head-on yet.

"You have to go," Micah said. "I had a healer look her over before bringing her here, and while I don't think the healer will say anything, anyone could have noticed us walking through the building. Besides, Verne is probably keeping an eye on me. I'm surprised he hasn't barreled in yet."

"Will you be all right?" Constantine asked, stepping closer.

Micah blinked as if he wasn't quite sure why Constantine was asking. "I'll be fine."

"You should come with us." Constantine wasn't supposed to offer that to Micah, but Mordred was worried, and he'd tried to convince Micah to leave the conclave several times already. Constantine doubted he'd get a different result, but he could try, especially considering the situation.

Just like Constantine expected, Micah shook his head. "I can't leave right now. They still don't know I'm working with you, and as long as they don't, I can still gather information and make sure you have everything. This is going to be vital for when the fighting starts."

"You already gave us a lot of information."

"I'm sorry, but I'm staying."

Constantine wanted to grab the stubborn man, throw him over his shoulder, and have Thor turn into smoke. Instead, he nodded curtly and turned to Marsha. "Do you need help getting up?"

She snorted and got to her feet. She swayed a little, but Micah was there, grabbing her elbow and keeping her upright. She nodded her thanks, then leaned closer to whisper something to him. Micah shook his head and gently guided her toward Thor.

Haven took her from Micah.

"Tell Mordred I'll contact him as soon as it's safe for me to," Micah said.

"I will. You're going to get in trouble for this."

"Probably, but I'm always getting in trouble for something. I'm the black sheep of the conclave, after all. Don't worry about me."

"How can we not?" Constantine asked. That drew Micah's attention to him. The way Micah was staring made Constantine want to shuffle his feet like a child, but he looked at the conclave member head-on.

Micah seemed amused. "I promised Mordred that I'd let him know if I'm in too much danger. I know what I'm doing, and I realize that if I'm killed, the conclave members will never pay for what they've done. I have every intention of changing the conclave so that it becomes what it was always supposed to be. That means not getting caught."

Constantine could do nothing but trust him. He took a step toward Thor, and Haven did the same, still clutching Marsha's arm. She looked confused, and Constantine could have sworn he heard her suck in a breath when they turned into smoke.

He glanced at Micah one last time. He understood what Micah had said about staying safe, but he wasn't sure Micah would have a choice. The other conclave members would be pissed when they found out that he'd taken Marsha out of her cell and that she'd vanished, and they'd blame him. Knowing them, they'd do everything they could to get Micah out of the conclave, and the easiest way to make that happen would be to kill him.

And Micah would be alone. He wouldn't have anyone there to protect him, which didn't sound fair to Constantine. He'd have offered to stay, but he'd be killed on sight. That would make Micah's life even more complicated, so instead of offering himself as a bodyguard, he allowed Thor to drift them away from Micah's office.

Hopefully, Constantine would see Micah again, and when he did, Micah would be in one piece.

For a few hours after Marsha had been taken away, Micah expected Verne and his friends to barge in, grab him, and lock him into the cell Marsha had been in earlier. He started relaxing when nothing like that happened, but he knew it wouldn't take long. What he'd done was unforgettable, and his hours at the conclave building were numbered.

So he did what he'd planned on doing when something like this happened. He copied everything he could from the computer and the database, hoping it would be enough to stop Verne and the others. Once he'd done that, he'd packed a few things that were now in a backpack by the door. Unfortunately for him, he couldn't turn to smoke like the others had earlier, which meant he'd have to get out of the building and create a portal so he could leave. It would be dangerous, but he had to hope he'd make it.

He wouldn't have it any other way.

He knew the time had come when he heard Daniel yell in protest at something that was happening just outside of Micah's office. This time, Micah hadn't locked the door, which meant that it swung in without resistance when Verne threw it open.

He, Elmer, and Hester strode toward Micah's desk. Since Micah had expected this, he'd taken a seat in a chair by the door. As soon as the three were inside his office, he got to his feet and placed himself between them and the open door.

"I thought that knocking was a basic sign of respect," he drawled.

"I'm sorry. I tried to stop them, but they didn't listen," Daniel said from behind Micah.

Micah didn't dare look away from Elmer and the other two for even a moment. "Don't worry about it, and get back to your desk."

"You don't deserve for us to knock on your door," Elmer snarled. "Where's Marsha? We know you took her away from her cell."

"I had a healer look her over. After what Verne did to her, it felt necessary."

Both Hester and Elmer glanced at Verne, looking surprised. It was enough to tell Micah that Verne hadn't been entirely honest with his friends.

Unfortunately, that didn't seem to be enough, and seconds later, their attention was on Micah again.

"You're going to tell us where she is," Hester said.

"Why would I do that? So Verne can torture her again?"

"We'll call for a meeting and vote on it. You shouldn't have taken her out without letting us know."

"I suppose I shouldn't have, but then Verne shouldn't have tortured her without telling all of us, either."

"Stop twisting this situation," Verne snapped.

He stepped closer to Micah, and Micah inched back toward the door. His backpack was right there, and it wouldn't take him more than a few seconds to grab it and run.

He didn't have a good answer to give them. He hadn't taken her back to the cell, and she wasn't in the infirmary. Even if they hadn't checked yet, it wouldn't take them long to do so, and then they'd know Micah had gotten her out. That was a clear sign of betrayal, and Micah would find himself in

Marsha's chair in the cell.

"She's safe," he said.

Verne's expression was triumphant. "You helped her escape. You're a traitor."

Micah drew himself straighter. This was it, but he wasn't done. Since he was about to run away, he had every intention of telling the three what he thought about them. "I did help her escape. What you were doing to her wasn't right. What you've been doing with all of this isn't right."

"When we find her, we'll put the two of you in neighboring cells so you can hear her scream as I torture her," Verne promised.

Micah shook his head. "You won't find her. I made sure of that." He swallowed. "The three of you have been twisting and changing what the conclave stood for. We were always supposed to protect both humans and supernatural creatures, but instead, you turned the heroes into an army that kills any supernatural creature on sight. You're using heroes to get what you want, to supply you with more power and riches, as if you didn't have enough already. You're not in this to protect humanity. You're in it to use it so you can get what you want."

Hester gaped. "How dare you?"

"I dare because I've been on the conclave for two hundred years, and you've always done this. I thought I could change things by becoming a conclave member, but I realized a long time ago that I couldn't because of the three of you. You'll never change. You're selfish monsters, and the only way to save the conclave and the heroes, and with them, the rest of the world, is getting rid of you."

"You're threatening us?" Verne asked.

"It's not a threat. It's a promise."

"I'll have you arrested and killed for this."

Micah had no doubt that would happen. He'd expected it

when he'd started this, and he was ready.

Before Verne could call for the guards, Micah grabbed his backpack, turned around, and ran. Daniel was standing in the middle of his office, looking worried, and his eyes widened when Micah whizzed past him.

Micah wished he could take Daniel with him, and he prayed he wouldn't get in trouble. He hadn't known anything about this, and hopefully, Verne and the others would believe him. No matter what Daniel told them, he wouldn't be putting Mordred and the fallen heroes in danger because he didn't know anything about what they'd been doing. He was innocent. The problem was that innocence had never mattered to Verne and his friends.

But this was the safest place for Daniel for the moment. Micah wasn't sure where he'd be going once he was out of here. It didn't matter, either. The only thing that did was that he had to get out of the building, and fast.

He ran through the hallways, ignoring the heroes he went past. No one tried to stop him, probably because they didn't know they should.

Micah managed to get out of the building. He stumbled as he rushed out the door, then grabbed the cell phone from his pocket. He'd left his conclave phone on his desk, but he'd grabbed the hidden one from the flower vase. He never stopped moving as he called Mordred to tell him what had happened. Mordred had promised that when the time came, he'd send people to help Micah and that he'd give Micah a safe place.

That was all Micah wanted. He'd spent years working against the other conclave members, and he was exhausted. During all those years, he'd been hypervigilant, had locked all his doors, and made sure that even when he slept, he'd be able to quickly act if something happened. He'd done what he had to do and had stayed with the conclave for as long as he could, but now, he was free.

Things would get worse before they got better. He had no doubt about that. The conclave would strike, and they would strike hard. It would get bloody, but Micah was ready to fight.

He was a conclave member, and his job was to protect the innocent from anyone who attacked them. Unfortunately, right now, it meant protecting them against heroes, too.

He'd do it. But first, he had to get out of here before Verne found him. He dialed the number he knew by heart and raised the phone to his ear as he looked around for a safe place where he could wait for a few moments.

Nowhere was safe, though, not while Verne, Elmer, and Hester were in control of the heroes.

When Constantine got another call from Mordred, he answered right away. He couldn't stop thinking about Micah and how they'd left him behind, and he knew it had to be the reason Mordred was calling.

"What is it?"

"My guy is in trouble."

Constantine had been hanging out in the living room, but he got up from the couch and headed out, barely waving back at his friends. They'd understand. It wasn't the first time Mordred called him for an urgent mission, and the same went for them. When Mordred called, they answered without hesitating.

"I'm heading outside right now," Constantine said. It would be no use to go to Mordred's office if he had to go outside to create a portal anyway.

"I'm calling Thor as soon as I hang up with you."

"What can we expect?"

"Micah didn't give me details when he called. He just said that he was on the run because something had happened. I think you'll have to fight, but I can't be sure."

"I'll be ready." And Constantine hoped Micah was okay.

It wouldn't be fair for something to happen to him after everything he'd done. He'd been stuck with the conclave all these years, trying to fix things but unable to. Now that he was finally free of them, he risked getting killed before he could do anything else.

He and Mordred hung up. Mordred had told Constantine where to go. Micah would be at the conclave building, and since there was no way Constantine was opening a portal inside of it, he'd arrive outside. Hopefully, Thor would be quick, and they'd be able to go right away.

He ran into the forest, ready to fight whoever stepped in his path. Thankfully, the few people he rushed past only gave him a few glances. By the time he reached the part of the forest they used to open portals, Thor was already there.

"Where did you come from?" Constantine asked as he threw out a hand to open the portal.

"I was down by the lake. Ready?"

"More than ever."

Constantine opened the portal. He waited until Thor had walked through to follow him, already looking for Micah when his feet landed in front of the conclave building. He could hear people fighting, but it was getting dark, and it took him a moment to find the source of the sounds. He wasn't surprised to find Micah fighting with two heroes when he did. Micah was clearly trying not to hurt them, which made sense, but the problem was that the heroes didn't seem to have the same problem. They weren't holding back, and Micah would get hurt if he wasn't careful.

Thor and Constantine looked at each other, then threw themselves into the fight.

Constantine grabbed one of the heroes by the arm and pulled her back. She squeaked in surprise, and Constantine took the opportunity to aim a punch at her nose. She ducked, grabbed his wrist, and pushed his arm up, but that didn't stop him. He kicked her in the stomach, and she stumbled back, a grimace on her face.

Constantine quickly looked around, relieved to see that Thor was handling the other hero. Micah was leaning against a nearby parked car, out of breath, a trickle of blood dripping from the corner of his mouth.

"Open a portal," Constantine ordered.

Micah nodded and threw his hand out. Before Constantine could say anything else, the hero attacked him again.

Heroes were trained to fight, and they used a specific kind of fighting skill that had been developed over the decades. They didn't usually fight each other, and the trainers were pretty rigid when it came to teaching the style to new heroes. Constantine hadn't been a hero in a while, and he'd learned new tricks.

When the hero rushed him, he waited until the last second, then he twisted on his feet, letting the hero rush past him. She tried to stop, but it took her a second, and Constantine used that second to his advantage. He kicked the hero off her feet, then before she could get up again, he knelt on her chest and punched her in the face.

It took a few punches, but she was eventually unconscious. Constantine waited one more second, but he knew they were out of time when he heard the building door open. More heroes were streaming out, ready to fight, and they were outnumbered.

Constantine ran toward Micah. He was in a defensive position, even though he was holding his arm close to his chest. He was clearly in pain, but he hadn't run away through the portal. Instead, he seemed ready to help Constantine and Thor, which was touching but unnecessary.

"Thor!" Constantine yelled.

"I'll be right there," Thor answered.

Constantine didn't wait for him. He grabbed Micah's arm and pushed him toward the portal, but Micah resisted.

"We can't leave him here."

"We're not leaving him. Just run through, please."

New screams made both of them turn around. Constantine's eyes widened at the sight that greeted him. He knew Thor had abilities he could only dream of. He was a draugr, and while they'd worked together a few times, Thor had only used a few of those abilities. Now, he was using another.

He'd shifted into a massive black bull, and he was charging two heroes. They weren't hanging around to see what would happen next. They started running toward the building, which gave Micah and Constantine a few seconds of reprieve. As much as Constantine wanted to keep staring, he pulled Micah toward the portal.

"See? He can take care of himself."

"That's incredible," Micah breathed out.

"And you can ask him all about his powers once we're home. Come on."

They walked through the portal. They only had to wait a few moments for Thor to come through, too. He was still in his bull form, and he was even more impressive from up close. He huffed and stomped his hooves on the ground as Micah made the portal vanish.

"What now?" Micah asked, sounding out of breath.

It was Constantine's turn to open a portal. "Now, we're taking you home."

Micah blinked. "I don't think I've had a place to call home in hundreds of years."

Mordred had told Constantine to bring Micah home when he came back. He trusted Micah enough to give him a room in the house they all lived in, which said a lot. Micah had been working for the fallen heroes for a long time, and he'd sacrificed so much. Now it was time for him to rest, at least for a few days.

The worst fight was still waiting for them, but they'd have time to deal with it.

The portal shimmered in front of them. Thor shifted back. Once he was in his human form, he offered Micah his hand. "We met when we came to get Marsha," he said.

Micah looked from Thor's hand to his face, and Constantine held his breath. Micah might be a good person, and he might have been helping the fallen heroes, but that didn't mean he wasn't wary of supernatural creatures. To Constantine's surprise, he eagerly took Thor's hand and shook it. "Micah."

"Thor."

"That was impressive. Can I ask what kind of creature you are?"

Constantine rolled his eyes. "Can we do this once we're home? I think Micah needs medical attention." He was still holding his other arm close to his chest, which Constantine suspected meant it was broken, or at the very least, injured. He was also still bleeding from his mouth, and Constantine hated to see his skin marred that way.

Thor snorted, but he took Micah's arm as they moved toward the second portal. He helped Micah through, and Constantine quickly followed them.

Once back in the forest, they had to walk a bit to get to the house. Constantine was tempted to ask Micah if he needed more help, but Thor seemed to have things in hand, and the two of them were talking as if they'd been friends for decades rather than having just met. Constantine quite enjoyed that fact. After everything Micah had done, he wanted the man to feel at home here. Still, he couldn't help but feel a little jealous. He wanted to be the one to help Micah. He wanted to be the one talking to him.

But that time would come. Micah was home now, and he was safe. In the end, that was all that mattered, and everything else could wait until he saw a healer, and they were sure he was okay.

CHAPTER FOUR

Micah didn't know where to start looking. He hadn't known what to expect when Thor and the fallen hero had appeared in the parking lot, but he was glad they had. He'd been holding his own, fighting with the two heroes, but he'd known more were coming. And even though he kept up with his training, he'd been a conclave member for a long time. He wasn't used to fighting anymore, which he supposed was why he'd gotten his arm broken.

Or at least he thought it was broken. It would be great if it wasn't, but it still hurt like hell.

Thankfully, he had people to support him. He'd been surprised to meet Thor. He'd seen the man when they'd rescued Marsha, and he'd been aware of the fact that the fallen heroes worked with several supernatural creatures, but he hadn't expected the man to volunteer to come to help him. After all, he was a conclave member. And the conclave had done so much damage to supernatural creatures in their communities. But from the way Thor was speaking, he didn't seem to hold it against Micah, which was both a relief and a surprise.

"I can also shift into a seal and a cat," he said as they walked toward the big house that Micah could see in the distance.

"That's impressive. I mean, I knew about it, but I've never seen it before."

Thor grinned. "You'll see lots now that we're home."

"Thank you for coming for me."

"How could we not? You've been helping us fight the

50

conclave. Now that you can't stay with them anymore, you're truly one of us."

Micah supposed that was true. He was a fallen hero now, too.

When one became a hero, there was no going back. Even after Micah had stopped going on missions and fighting and had become a conclave member, he'd still been a hero. He always would be until he died. There was no getting out of it, and he didn't want to. He still believed in the mission of the heroes. He wanted to protect the innocent, no matter what kind of creature they were.

And he would. As soon as the conclave had been dealt with, they'd build a new one, and this time, they'd do it the right way.

"Do you need someone to carry you?" the hero who was with them asked.

Micah turned his attention to him. He remembered him from before, but he hadn't seen this hero in a long time. The reason was obvious, since he was a fallen hero. "I can walk to the house," he said. "Can I get your name?"

The hero's cheeks flushed. "Sorry. I'm Constantine."

"It's a pleasure to see you again."

Constantine's eyes widened. "You remember me?"

"Vaguely. You haven't been a hero in a while, though."

"A few decades. I'm surprised you remember."

"I try to remember every hero, but it isn't easy."

Thankfully, they reached the house. Micah wanted to talk more to Thor and Constantine, but his arm hurt, and he couldn't wait to fall into bed. He'd been hypervigilant for so long that he felt he could sleep a week now and still wake up feeling tired.

Mordred was waiting for them on a large wooden deck in front of the house. He grinned when he saw Micah, but the grin quickly shifted to a frown when he noticed the way

Micah was holding himself.

"I'm fine," Micah promised.

"I'll be the judge of that, or rather, the healer will be. You're going straight to him."

Micah had expected that, but he hadn't expected Mordred to boss him around that way. "You can't give me orders."

Mordred grinned. "Can't I? Because here, you're not a conclave member. You're just another fallen hero, and I'm the boss."

Micah found himself laughing. "I see. Well, I can't say that's a lie. I suppose I'll see your healer."

"You'd better." Mordred's expression softened. "How are you?"

"I've been better, and I wish I didn't have to run, but I always knew this would happen one day."

"You're safe here with us."

"I have no doubt."

Mordred led the way inside the house. After a while, Thor disappeared, but Constantine stuck with Micah as they both followed Mordred. They didn't cross paths with anyone for a bit, but once they reached a deeper part of the house, Micah started seeing people. Most of the time, they gaped. Micah had no doubt they recognized him, and they had to wonder what he was doing here.

To Micah's surprise, he wasn't led to an infirmary. Instead, when they reached a room, it ended up being an office.

"We'll have more space and privacy to talk here," Mordred said. He gestured at the couch. "Sit down. I already texted our healer, and he'll be right here."

But Micah didn't think the healer was the man who stepped in, looking thunderous. "What is he doing here?" the man demanded to know.

He was a fallen hero, and Micah vaguely remembered him, but he couldn't remember his name. He looked at Constantine to ask, but Constantine's expression stopped him from saying anything. He looked pissed and ready to take the other fallen hero in a fight. Micah didn't want the fallen heroes to fight because of him.

"He's here because I offered him a place to stay," Mordred said. He sounded calm, very different than how Micah felt.

"He's a conclave member," the fallen hero spat out.

"He was working for us the entire time," Constantine intervened. "Just because you don't know about it doesn't mean it's a lie, Bowen. You've trusted Mordred until now. Why don't you continue doing so?"

Bowen looked from Micah to Constantine. They were sitting close. Constantine had been hovering around Micah since they'd crossed the first portal, as if he was afraid Micah would faint or hit his head if he wasn't there. Even though he didn't understand the other man's interest, Micah was touched.

"Trust you to pick up another stray," Bowen eventually said.

Constantine got to his feet while Micah blinked, trying to understand the words.

"Enough," Mordred snapped. "Bowen, Micah was a conclave member, but he's been working for us for decades. I won't have you pick a fight with him, especially when he's hurt."

"I got all the information I could before leaving," Micah stepped in, eager to show this hero that he could be trusted.

He wasn't an idiot. It would take a while for the fallen heroes to trust him, and he was ready to work for it. Mordred had kept the fact that he was helping the fallen heroes a secret, and Micah didn't regret that. It had kept both him and the fallen heroes safe. But it meant the fallen heroes had no idea of anything he'd done, and they viewed him as an enemy. Well, some of them did. Constantine didn't—but Bowen looked ready to kill.

Mordred gave Micah a gentle smile. "I'm not surprised you did. You put yourself in danger to get us what we needed, and I thank you for that." He turned his attention back to Bowen. "If I hear anything else from you, I'll have to punish you."

"How is this fair?" Bowen protested. "This is our home, and you're taking in people who don't deserve it."

"You can move out at any time if that's what you want. I'm not forcing anyone to live here, and I hope you remember that. Now, Micah needs food and rest, and I doubt he'll get any of that if you're here. If you have questions or doubts, you can come to my office tomorrow. In the meantime, you know where the door is."

Bowen looked like he wanted to protest, but instead, he glared at Micah one last time and turned around. He stomped out just as a man came in holding a black bag.

The man looked puzzled as he watched Bowen leave, but he quickly turned to Micah. "What happened?"

That was probably the healer. Micah settled against the couch, knowing it would take a while for the healer to be done with him. Constantine gave them space, and Micah didn't miss the way he slipped out the door. He wished Constantine had stuck around, but he understood the fallen hero had better things to do than babysit him.

He sighed. He was glad he'd managed to get away, but being here in this position unleashed emotions he hadn't felt in a long time. He didn't belong, and the situation was precarious. He'd have to convince everyone in the house he could be trusted, and if Bowen's reaction was anything to go by, it would take a lot of work.

Since the healer and Micah would be busy for a while,

Constantine ran after Bowen. He had something to say to his friend, and he didn't want Micah to hear.

"What the fuck are you doing?" he asked as soon as he was out the office door.

Bowen hadn't gone far. He was at the end of the hallway, and he stopped walking when he heard Constantine. He turned around to face him, and Constantine strode toward him.

"What do you think I'm doing? Mordred is bringing in enemies, and you don't see anything wrong with that?"

"Is this still about Percy? Because he's not our enemy. He's a fallen hero like you and me, and so is Micah."

Bowen snorted. "And you believe that? If you do, you're more stupid than I thought you were."

Constantine jerked back. Bowen hadn't hit him, but he might as well have. "What happened to you? Why did you become so bitter?"

Bowen shook his head. "I don't understand how you don't see it. Our mission will fail if Mordred continues bringing in people who shouldn't be here. I thought that was the most important thing for you—helping humanity the way we were supposed to all along."

"Of course it's important to me. But not everyone is an enemy. Hell, no one who lives here is. I know there have been many changes, but I don't get it. Other heroes have arrived before, and you've accepted them. What's the problem with Percy and Micah?"

Bowen stared for a moment before shaking his head. "You don't understand."

"I don't, but I want you to explain."

"Constantine?" Mordred asked from the office.

Constantine turned to find him standing at the door, waiting for him. "Yes?"

"I'd like you to come back once you're done."

"I'll be right there."

When he turned around to tell Bowen they'd talk later, it was too late. Bowen was gone, and Constantine was left standing alone in the hallway.

He sighed. He had no idea what happened to Bowen, but he wasn't sure he wanted to find out. He grieved the loss of one of his best friends, but he didn't have time for this. He, Mordred, and everyone else had other things to focus on, but Constantine hoped that if Bowen wanted to talk to him, he knew he could come anytime.

He doubted that would happen. The distance between them felt like too much, and he didn't think it could shrink.

He turned around and went back to the office. He didn't know if Bowen was a lost cause, but he didn't have the energy to beg his best friend to explain.

The healer was still talking to Micah when he got there, so he moved toward Mordred. "How is he?" he asked.

"From what I gathered, his arm isn't broken."

"That's good."

"It is. I'd like to ask you for a favor."

That got Constantine's attention. "Whatever you need." And he meant it. Mordred had given him a home and a purpose, and Constantine would do pretty much anything for the man.

"You know who Micah is and what he's done. I'd like you to keep an eye on him, especially the first few days. Maybe stick close to him. I can only imagine how hard it will be for him to go from being a respected conclave member to being just one of the fallen heroes. More importantly, many of the fallen heroes will have problems with his presence here. They don't trust him, and I don't blame them, since they didn't know what he was doing. I don't want him to be alone and feel like he's made the wrong decision by helping us."

"I'll stay with him." It wouldn't be a hardship. Constantine had so many questions for Micah, everything from why he'd decided to work against the conclave to what he was going to do now.

Micah and Mordred had plans for the conclave, but Constantine hadn't been told about them. He suspected that was about to change. But first, Micah deserved some time to rest. Waiting a week, or even longer, wouldn't change anything. The conclave wasn't going anywhere. If anything, the conclave would become even harsher now that Micah had been found out as a traitor and had run. Constantine wasn't looking forward to that, but maybe their subsequent actions would show the heroes who still worked for them what they'd become.

Mordred looked relieved. "Thank you."

"You don't have to thank me. I'd do this for anyone."

"You're a good man, Constantine. I'm glad I found you."

And Constantine was glad Mordred had found him.

He didn't know what he would have done if Mordred hadn't. After he and Bowen had left the conclave, they'd been lost. They'd stuck together because they hadn't known anything else, and they'd tried living a normal human life, but it hadn't been possible. They weren't human anymore. They were heroes, and they had a life mission they couldn't fulfill by hiding with humans. It had taken Mordred a few decades to find them, but when he had and offered them a place with him, Constantine had been relieved. Finally, he could do what he'd been trained to do — what he'd been born to do.

Help humanity.

The healer stepped away from Micah, and Mordred moved toward him. Since they were talking, Constantine decided to sit next to Micah. It had to be strange for him to be here. The conclave didn't go on missions as heroes did. They spent their time at the conclave building, barely leaving as far as Constantine could remember. And it wasn't just that. Micah had gone from being revered to being looked at with mistrust. He didn't deserve the hatred thrown at him, but it would take a while for the people in the house to warm up to him.

Constantine leaned closer to Micah. "How are you feeling?"

"Like I could sleep for a week."

"Well, I can't promise you a week, but as soon as everything is over here, I'll take you to one of the guest rooms." Constantine would make sure to choose one out of the way so Micah wouldn't be bothered by the other heroes. Even though he was one of them now, he needed his privacy.

"Thank you," Micah said. "And not just for the guestroom offer. You saved my ass."

And what a nice ass it was. "You needed help, and I was there. I couldn't have looked the other way."

Micah was pale, and his smile was tremulous, but it was there. "Well, thank you anyway. It means a lot to me that you helped me and that you don't mistrust me like I'm sure everyone else in the house does."

"That's because I knew about you. I'm friends with Percy, the fallen hero you helped out of the conclave building recently."

"I remember him. I'm glad he made it home in one piece."

"Only thanks to you. I'm sure as soon as everyone finds out what you did, they'll be welcoming. If they manage to share living spaces with supernatural creatures they were trained to kill, I don't see why you should be a problem."

"I have so many questions," Micah murmured.

Constantine found himself smiling. Micah reminded him of himself when he'd first arrived here. He'd had so many questions that he'd been sure someone would kick him out just to make him shut up. "I'll answer any question you have tomorrow once you've gotten some rest."

"I see I'll have to get used to being ordered around."

"You'd better. Mordred is the boss, and everyone agrees on that." But Constantine couldn't deny the fact that he wanted to protect Micah. It wasn't just because Micah had a fragile beauty to him. It was also because he looked as if he hadn't had a good night's sleep in decades. His gray eyes were circled with dark bruises, and his hair was everywhere. He was too thin, as if he forgot to eat regularly, and Constantine promised himself he'd make sure that didn't happen here.

He wasn't Micah's friend yet, but he could see that changing. Micah would need support, especially in the first few weeks, and Constantine would be there to provide it. He'd provide Micah with anything he needed, and he'd protect him from any fallen hero who, like Bowen, had something to say about his presence here.

He'd be Micah's shield against the darkness of his old life for as long as Micah needed him to be.

Micah had hoped he'd be able to get some sleep as soon as possible, but he realized that wasn't going to happen when someone knocked on the office door right after the healer had left.

"Yes?" Mordred called out.

The door opened, and Micah's eyes widened when he saw who was standing there.

Thor was present, which was a relief, since Micah already knew him, but he wasn't alone. A grumpy blond man stood next to him with his arm protectively wrapped around the shoulders of a more petite, delicate-looking man. On Thor's other side was a man with red eyes that betrayed his status of a mage.

But the red-eyed man wasn't the strangest-looking person waiting to come in. Micah recognized a leshy hovering right behind Thor, next to Haven. Percy was there, along with another man, and, finally, a beautiful blond who pushed past them, headed right for Mordred.

Micah did a quick headcount, coming up with nine people. They'd fit in the office, but it would be a tight fit.

He hadn't expected to be talking to so many people as soon as he'd arrived, but he was fascinated by the fact that several of them were supernatural creatures.

Even though he believed supernatural creatures should be protected like anyone else and that heroes should take care of them instead of killing them, he hadn't had much contact with their community. It would have been too suspicious, and besides, conclave members rarely left the conclave building. The only people Micah had connections with regularly were heroes and other conclave members and, on the phone, Mordred.

Things were different here, and while Micah couldn't wait to see what would happen next, he also wished he could go to bed.

Mordred wrapped his arm around the beautiful blond and pulled him close, kissing his forehead. Then he turned to Micah. "I know you probably want to go to bed, but I'd like to introduce you to a few friends. Most of the fallen heroes in the house will be wary of you, but everyone in this office welcomes you." He paused and looked at the grumpy blond. "Well, except Tryg, but he doesn't welcome anyone but Isaac."

The shorter blond next to the grumpy guy who seemed to be Tryg chuckled and stepped toward Micah. Tryg was right behind him, hovering close as if he expected Micah to attack him. He didn't seem friendly, but at least Mordred had warned Micah.

"I'm Isaac," the shorter man said softly. "And Tryg is my boyfriend. And don't worry about him. He's grumpy, but he won't hurt you."

Micah nodded. By the time everyone had introduced them-selves, his head spun, and he felt stunned and happy at the same time. He couldn't wait to talk to all of them and find out about their lives, but he felt like he was about to fall asleep right here on the couch, and he doubted that would leave a good impression.

"I knew you worked with supernatural creatures, but I didn't expect this," he told Mordred.

Mordred's arm was wrapped around his boyfriend's shoulders. Apparently, Amyas was an undine, which ex-plained his beauty.

"They don't normally live here with us, but considering what's happening, we thought it would be safer."

"And the only one who had a problem with that is Tryg, but we don't listen to him," Thor added.

Tryg glared at him, but Thor didn't seem to care.

"I'm glad you managed to fix some of the wrongs the con-clave has done over the decades," Micah said. "I've been do-ing what I can, but I couldn't reach out to the supernatural community."

"You've done more than enough."

And his night wasn't over.

Micah sucked in a breath. "I need to tell you what hap-pened, but first, I'd like to know if Marsha is okay."

Mordred settled on the couch in front of the one Micah was sitting on. Everyone took a seat in the room, and Micah couldn't miss the fact that Tryg and Isaac were closer to the desk than to the rest of them, as if Tryg expected one of them to hurt his boyfriend. Micah was sure he had a good reason to be overprotective, and he wasn't about to poke that bear.

"She's fine," Mordred promised. "The healer checked her when she arrived, and you got to her in time. The only thing Verne managed to do was hit her a few times."

It was still a few times too many, but Micah was relieved.

"Is she here?"

"She is. We thought it would be best for her to stay at the house, although she's in pretty much the same place you're in. Many of the fallen heroes don't trust her. Not that she seems to care."

Micah chuckled. "She's not the type."

He was very much aware of the fact that Constantine was sitting next to him. The man hadn't said much since the group of people had arrived, but every time Micah glanced at him, Constantine was looking at him as if he was afraid something would happen to him. It reminded Micah of Tryg and Isaac, although he didn't understand why Constantine was behaving this way. He couldn't say he was sorry about it. It felt good to have someone care about him this way, even though Mordred had probably ordered Constantine to keep an eye on him. Constantine couldn't care about Micah when they barely knew each other.

"What happened, then?" Mordred asked.

"Marsha was the straw that broke the camel's back. I knew this could happen when I got her out, but I didn't have a choice. Verne had decided she needed to die, and you remember how he is."

Mordred grimaced. "Unfortunately, I do."

"Since I expected it, I copied every new file I could find on the network. It's all in the external memory I gave you. Unfortunately, I won't be able to do anything else now that I'm out."

"You've done more than enough. No one would berate you for taking a step back and staying out of the fight."

"I won't be doing that. I've been working for too long to take out the conclave. I'll be there when it happens." Micah swallowed. "Verne, Elmer, and Hester came to my office. Since I expected it, I managed to place myself between them and the door. Verne threatened me, and I'm pretty sure he already knew I was working against the conclave. He didn't have any proof, so he couldn't do anything about it. But he confronted me, and after getting Marsha out, I knew that I would end up in a cell. So I told Verne and the others what I thought about them, then I ran."

Percy sucked in a breath. "That took some courage."

Micah smiled at him. "Not as much as you'd think. Verne and his friends haven't given me orders in a long time, and I've worked with them as an equal for just as long. Besides, I know how horrible they are. It felt good to tell them they were assholes to their faces, to be honest. I'm just sorry I won't be able to help the fallen heroes from the inside anymore."

"I'd tell you you've done more than enough again, but I doubt you'd listen," Mordred said.

"Anyway, on the external memory I gave you is a list of heroes who have recently deserted the conclave. They never came back after their missions, and I think it's safe to say that the video you emailed everyone is working. You might be able to contact them, but I can't help you there."

"We'll go over it and see what we can do." Mordred got to his feet. "Now, I'm sure you can't wait to get some rest. Constantine will show you to a guest room and make sure you have everything you need."

Micah could have kissed Mordred, but instead, he stood up. His legs felt shaky, both from the exhaustion and the adrenaline of the fight leaving his body. He was going to crash, and soon, and he hoped he'd be on his own when it happened.

He looked at the people sitting in the room. "Thank you for welcoming me here. I know that for some of you especially, it wasn't easy, but I promise that we'll take the conclave down. They haven't been doing their job for several hundreds of years, and now, the time has come for them to pay."

And it was about time.

Constantine was surprised that Micah hadn't fallen on his face yet. He looked like he might fall asleep as he walked, which was why Constantine hovered close by as he led him through the house.

They were on the ground floor, and since they were walking past several rooms, he decided he might as well point them out. He doubted Micah would remember half of it by the time he woke up tomorrow, but Constantine wouldn't mind telling him again.

"Why don't we stop in the kitchen?" he suggested, gently cupping Micah's elbow and guiding him in that direction. "I don't know if you're hungry, but even if you're not, you can grab some snacks and a few bottles of water to keep in your room. That way, when you wake up, you'll have something to eat."

Micah blinked as if he couldn't quite understand what Constantine was saying. "Thank you." he eventually said.

"It's not a problem. I remember being where you are. Well, it wasn't exactly the same, of course, but coming here was overwhelming. I can only imagine how much worse it is in your position."

"I knew this would happen sooner rather than later."

"Doesn't mean it's easy."

Thankfully, the kitchen was empty except for a few heroes who seemed curious rather than angry at Micah's presence. They didn't ask questions, and Constantine nodded in thanks. He had no doubt that half of the house knew about Micah's presence by now, but Micah wasn't in any shape to answer questions. The only thing he was in shape to do was go to bed. So as soon as Constantine had grabbed several packets of saltines, a few bottles of water, and an entire box of cereal, he guided Micah out of the kitchen.

Micah seemed to be leaning more heavily against Constantine, and Constantine took the opportunity to grab his backpack from his hand. He'd been dragging it since they'd left the office.

Micah didn't protest. He blinked up at Constantine, his expression sleepy. Constantine stuffed the food into the backpack without looking at what else was inside, then he wrapped his arm around Micah's shoulders and pulled him close.

"We're almost there," he promised, hoping he wasn't being creepy.

He couldn't deny he wanted Micah close. He was fascinated by the man, and like every other fallen hero in the house, he had dozens of questions. The difference was that they weren't all about what Micah had done with the conclave and his situation here. He wanted to ask Micah when he was born and where he'd grown up. He wanted to know if Micah had left a special someone behind. The conclave had rigid rules that the heroes couldn't fraternize, but they didn't always follow those rules. Micah might have left someone he cared about behind, and while the thought made Constantine sad, he also realized it might give him an advantage. He was here, while this hypothetical person wasn't.

He was an asshole. He shouldn't be thinking about getting in Micah's bed.

"That's the living room, and that's the downstairs bathroom," he said as they walked toward the stairs. "Generally, you can go into whatever room you want to go in on the ground floor. There are mostly bedrooms on the other floors, though, so you should knock and wait for whoever is inside to tell you whether or not you can go in."

"I won't be doing any exploring anytime soon," Micah murmured.

"Probably not, but I thought you should know. We're a

tight group, and Mordred was right when he said it's going to take a while for people to warm up to you, but I know they will."

"How can you be so sure?"

"You're a great guy, and you've done a lot for our fight. When they find out, they'll welcome you, just like I have." Except for a few people, one of them being Bowen. Constantine was convinced there was something more to Bowen's behavior, but he couldn't put his finger on it, and frankly, he was tired of trying.

If Bowen wanted to talk to him, he would. In the meantime, Constantine would keep his distance from his friend, mostly because he was in no mood to start fighting with him.

"Marsha is okay?" Micah asked.

"She is. She's staying in one of the rooms close to yours, so you'll be able to talk to her if you want. I'm pretty sure she's already asleep, though."

"That's fine. I just needed her to be okay."

"She is, and so are you."

"That's a miracle."

Constantine agreed. So many things could have gone wrong. But Micah had made it out alive and in one piece, and that was all that mattered.

They finally reached the guestroom. Constantine threw the door open, turned the light on, and looked around to make sure Micah would have everything he'd need. They kept the guestrooms stocked up for new fallen heroes, so Constantine knew there would be soap and shampoo in the shower and fresh clothes in the dresser. It probably wasn't what Micah was used to, but hopefully, it would be enough.

He stepped in and put the backpack on the bed before turning to Micah. "This will be your room for as long as you want. If you need anything, feel free to find me. I'll help you as well as I can. The bathroom is through the door, and you're welcome to come downstairs and grab food anytime you want."

"Whatever you picked up from the kitchen will be fine for a while."

Constantine expected that answer. If he were in Micah's place, he wouldn't want to face the fallen heroes just now, either. "I'm going to give you my phone number," he said, reaching for a notepad on the desk by the window. "Call me anytime, even if it's two AM. I could tell you how to get to my room, but I'm pretty sure you'd get lost, so this is easier. Don't worry about bothering me, because you won't."

"I'm not sure I understand why you're so nice."

Constantine didn't, either. Since Micah seemed to want an answer, he had to come up with something. It wasn't that hard. "I've been with the fallen heroes for a few decades. I've had to fight against other heroes, and it broke my heart every time. I understand why some of them couldn't see that what the conclave was doing was wrong. After you've been told for hundreds of years that you're on the right side of the fight and that the conclave knows better, it isn't easy to let go of that. But the fight wouldn't be where it is now if it weren't for you, and I'm grateful for that. We all are."

"Thank you. I didn't do anything incredible, though. You and the other fallen heroes have been fighting all along while I've been sitting on my ass."

"You've been putting your life in danger for decades. Don't downplay that. And get some sleep. You look like you're about to fall on your face."

Micah laughed, and the humor made him look ten years younger. "I feel that way. I appreciate the compliment, though."

Constantine made sure Micah didn't need anything else one more time, then he left.

He wanted to stay, but there was nothing else he could do

for Micah tonight. Hopefully, tomorrow morning, Micah would feel better, and everyone in the house would know what he'd done. Micah would always have a place with them, even though he wasn't aware of that yet.

Constantine would make sure of that.

CHAPTER FIVE

Micah was finally free.

He didn't fully realize that until the next morning. When he woke up in a room he'd never been in and in a bed that wasn't his, he was confused for a few seconds. Then the pain in his arm reminded him of what had happened yesterday.

He'd left the conclave. He'd stood up to them, had told them what he thought of them, then he'd run. He'd been lucky that Mordred had been there to catch him and even luckier to make it out alive.

But he had, and he was free. There would be no more conclave meetings, no more fighting with Verne and his people because of the orders they were giving. Micah would still try to protect supernatural creatures, but he'd have to find other ways to do it, because he wasn't a conclave member anymore. If anything, he was the conclave's enemy.

A fallen hero.

After getting up, he'd showered, put on some of the clothes he'd found in the dresser, and now he was ready for more. He was hungry, and he knew he and the others had a lot of work to do, but he was still at his bedroom door, wondering what was next.

Could he really go downstairs, find the kitchen again, and sit there as if nothing had happened? Both Mordred and Constantine had told him he was welcome to whatever he wanted from the kitchen, but it felt like he didn't belong here. He had no doubt that whatever fallen hero he crossed paths with would have something to say about his presence, and he wasn't sure he could face that just yet. Most of the people in this house wouldn't be happy to see him, and he'd leave as soon as he could, but it would be sometime before the conclave could be replaced and the old members put on trial. In the meantime, he wasn't going anywhere.

He supposed the others would have to get used to that.

After sucking in a breath, Micah left his bedroom. The hallway was empty, which gave him a few moments of reprieve, but it didn't last long. As soon as he found the stairs and walked down, he encountered two fallen heroes.

They were talking to each other, but they both froze when they saw him. They stared, which Micah despised, so he tried to smile and wave at them. He remembered where the kitchen was, but he supposed he could ask them anyway. "Good morning. Can you remind me where the kitchen is?"

One of the fallen heroes kept staring, but the other one gave him a tremulous smile and pointed down the hallway. "It's down there, and if you're quick, you can get pancakes. There were some left when we left the kitchen."

"Thank you."

The fallen hero hesitated. "I remember you, you know?" she asked.

Micah wasn't surprised. "I hope it's good memories."

"There are no good memories when it comes to the conclave, but everyone here knows you've been working with us for years, and I wanted to thank you. You put yourself in danger in a way that none of us can fully understand."

Micah hadn't done it to be thanked, but her words still made his eyes prickle with tears he didn't want to shed. "Thank you. I only did what was right. I was in a unique position, and I used it."

She nodded. "Yes, well, I look forward to working with you."

"Just as I look forward to working with you and the other fallen heroes."

Micah wandered toward the kitchen, still thinking about the conversation. It was good to know that some of the fallen heroes didn't hate him and were even looking forward to working with him. He hadn't thought that would be the case, and it made him feel better about his choice to stick around. Things would have been much harder to work through if he'd had to find another place to stay.

He was distracted, which was why he didn't notice the man standing just inside one of the doors he walked by. The man grabbed his arm—thankfully, the good one—and dragged Micah into the room. Micah looked around for a few seconds, just long enough to realize it was a small sitting room, then he looked at the man who'd pulled him inside.

It was Bowen.

Micah remembered him from yesterday, so he knew it wouldn't be a nice conversation. Hopefully, Bowen wouldn't start a fight, but Micah wouldn't put it past him considering his thunderous expression.

"Yes?" Micah asked as if Bowen hadn't just been incredibly rude.

The fallen hero glared at him. "What are you doing here?" he demanded to know.

"I thought you were informed of that yesterday. I'm here to help in the fight against the conclave."

Bowen sneered. "Don't lie to me. I'm not an idiot like everyone else. I don't trust you."

"That's certainly your prerogative. The fact that you don't trust me doesn't change what I'm here for, though."

"You're spying for the conclave, aren't you? You're going to tell them everything about the fallen heroes and this home, and then they'll attack us."

"I'm not. I might not have known where the house was

until I arrived here, but I knew a lot about the fallen heroes. After all, I provided you with most of the information you used to fight the conclave and its heroes. If I wanted to tell the other conclave members about you and what you were doing, I would have done so a long time ago. I could also have created a trap and had the conclave capture you, yet you're still here."

"I don't care what you're saying. I don't trust you."

"You've already mentioned that. I don't need you to repeat it, because I heard you the first time." Micah realized he was pushing, but Bowen irritated him.

He'd never expected the fallen heroes to trust him, but he did expect them not to drag him into rooms to threaten him. Bowen hadn't said much beyond what he thought Micah was doing, but his stance and the way he hovered over Micah were enough for Micah to be sure this was a threat.

Micah had to work with what he had, no matter how limited. He couldn't afford to antagonize anyone, not even Bowen. He cleared his throat. "I understand why you don't trust me. You didn't know that I was working with Mordred the entire time and feeding him information about the conclave and the missions. I don't take the fact that you don't trust me personally, and I realize that even when things change, there's no way everyone here can like me. I won't do anything to hurt the fallen heroes, though. As I said, if I wanted to do that, I would have a long time ago."

Bowen's eyes narrowed. "Nothing you say will change my mind."

Micah shrugged. "I had to try. Besides, there has to be a reason you dragged me into this room."

"I say it's because he's an idiot," a new voice said from the door.

Both Bowen and Micah turned to look at the new arrival. Micah was relieved when he recognized Amyas, but Bowen appeared even more angry than he had before.

"Why are you defending him?" he snapped.

"Because, unlike you, I have faith in Mordred."

"I never said I didn't have faith in him," Bowen protested.

"You might not have said it, but your actions speak louder than your words. Mordred told you that while you didn't have to like Micah, you have to trust him. He has a lot more information than you can ever have about the conclave and what Micah did. Why did you corner Micah? Isn't it because you don't trust Mordred's opinion of him?"

Bowen opened his mouth, but instead of saying something more, he shook his head and pushed past Amyas. He rushed away, leaving Micah wondering what had just happened.

He'd known some of the fallen heroes wouldn't like the fact that he was here and that they'd have something to say about it, but he was starting to wonder if maybe he should leave. Bowen had looked like he wanted to punch him, which Micah couldn't say he was looking forward to.

Amyas sighed. "You have to excuse Bowen. He's jealous."

Micah blinked. "I'm sorry?"

Amyas gestured toward the hallway, and Micah followed him there. "You're going to the kitchen, yes?" he asked.

"I was. I thought I could grab something to eat."

"I'll make sure you get there without anyone else dragging you into side rooms. As I was saying, though, I think Bowen is jealous."

"I don't understand what he's jealous of."

"He's Constantine's best friend, and he had to watch as Constantine became friends with Percy. Percy is our more recent fallen hero, and he arrived only a couple of months ago, if even that. He and Constantine became fast friends, and Bowen doesn't like that. It looks to me like he might have transferred some of that jealousy onto you."

Micah had no idea what that meant, but he hoped it

wouldn't create even more problems for him. He already had enough of those without adding a jealous friend to the pile.

Constantine could have cheered when Amyas and Micah came into the kitchen. He hadn't been sure if he should go to Micah's bedroom and ask him if he wanted breakfast brought upstairs to him, or maybe if he wanted a guide to the kitchen, so he hadn't done either of those things. He hadn't even been sure Micah was awake yet, but obviously, he was.

He and Amyas were talking as they walked, but the conversation ended quickly, probably because Micah realized that everyone in the kitchen was staring at him. He raised his head high, facing the few fallen heroes still eating, and nodded at them. "Good morning," he said.

A few fallen heroes looked shocked, but most said good morning back. Constantine bounced on his seat. And when Micah looked at him, he patted the one next to him. "Come sit with me," he said.

Micah peered back at Amyas, who seemed amused and gestured at him to go. He was hesitant as he walked toward Constantine, and Constantine hoped it didn't have to do with him. It probably didn't. Micah was new, and he could no doubt use a friendly face. Constantine was happy to be that face.

"What do you want to eat?" he asked once Micah was next to him.

"Whatever is easier. I don't need anyone to go to any trouble for me."

"It wouldn't be a trouble. It was Lilith's turn to cook this morning, and she made pancakes. There are some left in the oven if you want them."

"Pancakes would be wonderful."

Constantine hopped up and rushed to the oven. He quickly

grabbed the plate inside, moved some pancakes from it to a new plate, then picked up silverware and a napkin and went back to Micah. There was already a mug in front of him, and someone had filled it with coffee, possibly Amyas, who was sitting on the other side of the table now.

He and Micah were talking, and Constantine liked the smile on Micah's face. It was better than how it had looked yesterday, with blood dripping down his lips.

"Here you go," he said as he placed the plate in front of Micah.

Micah tilted his head up, smiling at Constantine in a way that made Constantine's heart race.

"Thank you," Micah said.

"You're welcome." He sat down in his chair again. "So, how was your night?"

"Better than I expected. I slept very well."

"How come you didn't give *me* pancakes?" Amyas asked with a whine. Constantine's eyes widened and he started to get to his feet, but Amyas shook his head and gestured at him to sit back down. "Don't worry about it. I'll grab something myself."

Constantine moved his attention back to Micah. "You're different," he said.

Micah paused as he was about to eat a bite of pancake from his fork. "What do you mean?"

"From the other conclave members. I mean, there's no way you're the only one who realizes that what they're doing is wrong, right?"

Micah sighed and leaned back in his chair. "I don't think I am. There are at least another two conclave members I think the fallen heroes could work with. They're uncomfortable with what the conclave does, but we had a minority even with me. We couldn't go against what Verne and his friends did."

"Which is why you worked against him from the inside."

"Exactly. I suppose that's over now."

"Well, you did tell the other conclave members they were assholes, so I think it is. That's not what I meant when I said that you're different, though."

"What did you mean?"

Constantine tried to put his thoughts into words. "Why are you the only one who did something about it? I mean, even though two conclave members dislike what's happening, I doubt they've helped us or anyone else. So, they understand this is wrong, but it's not enough for them to do something about it. But for you, it was."

"I think there are a few reasons for that. I'm the most recent conclave member. I've only been with them a few hundred years, and I already had problems with what the conclave was doing before I became one of them. I went into this knowing what I wanted to do, and while I've had to change things because it didn't work the way I thought it would, I still want to change the conclave. But because of this and how recent I am, I don't feel the need to cling to my position the way the others do. Some of them have been on the conclave for so long that I wonder if they even know what they are beyond a conclave member. It's become their entire life, and it's hard for them to let it go."

"What's next?" Amyas asked as he sat back down in his chair. He'd grabbed a plate that was heavy with a high pile of pancakes that he proceeded to drown in half a bottle of syrup.

"I'm not entirely sure," Micah said. "I suppose I should find Mordred and talk to him. He'll be able to tell me what he expects from me and what our next step will be."

"This is going to be very different from what you're used to," Constantine said.

"It will be, but I don't see that as a bad thing. It was time for things to change. I'm sorry I won't be able to help the fallen heroes from the inside anymore, but it doesn't mean I won't be doing anything. I have every intention of fighting by your side and doing everything I can to bring down the conclave and create a better one."

Amyas hummed. "So you believe there should be a conclave, just not the one that's already in place."

Micah sighed. "If we want heroes to protect humanity, there has to be someone who governs them. Otherwise, it would be chaos, and the heroes would be unable to find the people they need to protect. The conclave was a good idea when it was first created, but that was thousands of years ago. Things have changed, and we should have changed with them, but we didn't, and this is the result."

Amyas pointed his fork at Micah. "Well, whatever the next step will be, I think you should make yourself comfortable. Not everyone dislikes you as much as Bowen does. This is your home now, and I want you to *feel* like it is."

Constantine had no idea what Amyas was talking about, and while he wanted to ask, he suspected that wouldn't be the brightest idea. If Amyas or Micah wanted him to know, they'd tell him. He supposed he could go to Bowen and ask him, but that was the last thing he wanted to do.

"I'll show you around again," he offered. "I'm sure you have a meeting with Mordred, but if this is going to be your home, you should know where everything is, right?"

A smile played on Amyas's face, and he arched a brow in question when Constantine looked at him. Constantine shrugged, unsure of what Amyas wanted to hear from him. He'd always been the friendly type, and he'd done the same when it came to Percy. There was no difference, even though Micah had been a conclave member.

Micah smiled gently. "I'd be happy to get a tour of the house. You're right when you say that if I'm going to live here, I should know where everything is. There's no better way for me to find out than have someone who's lived here for a while show me, right?"

"You should do that after breakfast," Amyas said. "In the meantime, I'll go find Mordred and ask him what he wants you to do today. You'll probably have a meeting with him later, but I doubt he'll expect you to go to him right away. There should be time for a thorough tour of the house."

Constantine had no idea what Amyas was doing, but it seemed like he was pushing him and Micah together, and he was grateful. He wanted to spend more time with Micah and show him that not every fallen hero was rude like Bowen had been yesterday.

He wanted Micah to feel welcome and like this place could become his home, and he'd do anything to make that happen.

Micah knew he should go to work right away, but he was glad for the respite. It wouldn't be long, anyway. No matter how big the house was, they couldn't exactly spend the entire day walking through it.

But following Constantine around made Micah feel better. There would be time for meetings and deciding what was next. He could waste a few hours thinking only about Constantine and how nice he was.

"So, the house is big," Constantine was saying. "Not every fallen hero lives with us, though. I think for some of them, it was better to get a place outside of it. We were forced to live together as heroes, and they wanted things to be different."

"That's understandable," Micah murmured.

Constantine grinned. "I guess it is, but I like living here. It's nothing like living in the conclave building was. For one, there's a pool."

Micah found himself laughing. "I take it you enjoy swimming?"

"I love swimming. During the summer, I swim in the lake,

but it gets too cold in the winter. That's where the pool comes in."

"Will you show me the pool?"

Constantine grinned. "I thought you'd never ask. Come on."

Micah could only follow Constantine. The fallen hero was bouncy, and he seemed happy every time Micah saw him, which made Micah smile. The situation was dire, but that apparently wasn't enough to get Constantine to stop smiling.

There would be pain and blood before all of this was over, but Micah prayed that Constantine's smile would never vanish.

"So I don't know what happened between you and Bowen, but from what Amyas said, something did?" Constantine asked as they walked through the house.

"You and Bowen are friends?" If that was the case, Micah didn't want to say anything that would break their friendship.

"I'm not sure anymore. I mean, we were partners with the heroes, and we left together, but he's been behaving strangely. We were close until recently when Percy arrived. For some reason, Bowen is pissed that I'm Percy's friend, and I'm pissed that he's pissed and rude about it."

"I'm sorry your friendship is troubled."

"I can't say I'm not, but maybe it was time for us to take a step back from each other. Friendships don't last forever, do they? We're different people from how we were when we were with the conclave, so it makes sense. I just don't like how bitter he's been and how he can't see that both you and Percy are good people and working with us and not for the conclave."

Micah understood the drifting away and losing friendships. After all, he was hundreds of years old, and he'd lost his fair share of people. For some reason, though, he didn't want Constantine to have to suffer through it. He never wanted the smile on Constantine's face to fade, even though he realized it was an impossibility. No one could be happy all the time, not even people who seemed to be.

But Micah liked Constantine, and he could see them becoming friends. That would have been a forbidden thought if he'd still been with the conclave, but now, nothing stopped them from becoming close.

It was an odd feeling. Micah had been on his own for as long as he could remember, first as a hero, then as a conclave member. Some of the other conclave members were friends, but he'd never fit with any of them. Verne, Hester, and Elmer were monsters, and Micah had never wanted to be their friend. He'd hoped that things would be different with Johnson and Claire, but they hadn't welcomed him with open arms. They were close to each other, having been on the conclave for almost the same length of time. But Micah had always been an outsider, much like Kalliope.

And now, here he was. His life had changed over just a few hours, and he didn't know what to do with himself. He had freedom, but there was so much of it that it was almost scary.

But as he watched Constantine excitedly show him the house, pointing out things and telling him small anecdotes about his friends, he could see this becoming his life. He hadn't betrayed the conclave and worked with the fallen heroes for himself, but he couldn't deny this was a nice secondary effect.

Constantine was one of the people Micah would've watched from afar before, yearning to become their friend or at least talk to them. Now, he had the possibility of doing just that, but he wasn't sure he could. He didn't have friends. He didn't know how to deal with friendship, and he didn't understand how Constantine could accept him so easily. It was much easier to understand why Bowen couldn't, but maybe it was time to let go of all of that. He wasn't a conclave member anymore. He was a fallen hero, and he deserved some happiness in his life. If that happiness came through Constantine, who was Micah to argue and say it wasn't good?

"I know you haven't brought much with you, so you probably have to go shopping," Constantine was saying. "At the very least, you need to buy a bathing suit. Or you could swim naked, but only in the lake. We can't do that in the pool."

He looked a bit grumpy, which told Micah there was a good reason for that. "Has anyone tried swimming in the pool naked?"

"We're all adults here! I don't see why anyone would have a problem with me swimming naked, especially when I'm the only one in the pool."

Micah almost laughed. "Indeed. So I'm guessing this rule was created because of you?"

"Yeah. I don't swim in the pool naked anymore, so you don't have to worry."

Micah wasn't worried. If anything, he wouldn't mind seeing Constantine naked.

He blinked. It had been a while since he was last attracted to someone and even longer since he'd allowed himself to do anything about it. As a conclave member, he rarely left the building, which meant there was little chance for a relationship or even flings.

But Constantine was cute. His brown eyes sparkled with mischief and happiness, and there was a red streak in his brown hair. He kept his hair long to his shoulder, very different from the conclave rules. He was slightly shorter than Micah, and while he trained, since he was a fallen hero, he wasn't overly muscled. He looked like he'd fit nicely against Micah's body, and for the first time in a while, there was a possibility of that happening.

Micah hadn't missed the way Constantine kept peeking at him as they walked and talked. He was pretty sure

Constantine was interested in him, and he was interested in Constantine. Micah didn't want to push, but he was curious to see where things would go between them, and it was freeing to know that something *could* happen.

Constantine showed Micah the pool, and then the gym, the games room, and every other room Micah might need. Micah was overwhelmed by the time they were done, and he was almost relieved when Constantine mentioned they should head toward Mordred's office.

"I should probably talk to him," he agreed.

"The two of you will want to start talking about what's next for the conclave and its members."

"I'm sure he has plans." Mordred always did.

Constantine chuckled. "He knows what he's doing."

Micah doubted anyone did in this situation, but he found himself nodding. Mordred knew what he was doing better than Micah, which was all that mattered.

Micah wasn't a conclave member anymore. He was a fallen hero. And to be honest, he was relieved to give up the authority he'd carried since he'd become a conclave member. It had never done any good. He'd never wanted it, and now he could give it up and follow a man who was better suited to be a leader than he ever had been.

The final destination of the tour ended up being Mordred's office. Constantine wanted to keep talking to Micah, but now wasn't the time. Mordred and Micah had no doubt many things to say to each other, and while Mordred hadn't called yet, he would eventually. It was time for Constantine to let go of Micah, and he found that he didn't want to.

He liked Micah. In the beginning, he'd only been curious, but that had changed. He was still curious because he barely knew anything about Micah, but now, he liked him because of the kind of person he was.

He'd sacrificed hundreds of years and had put himself in danger of being found out as a traitor, all because he wanted to do the right thing. Bowen might not believe that was what Micah had been doing, but Constantine did, and he was in awe.

He stopped in front of Mordred's office door and turned to Micah. "Well, here it is."

Micah looked around. "I recognize it from yesterday."

"It's probably going to take you a while to get used to the house and not get lost on your way to the kitchen, but if you need anything, including a tour guide, call me. You still have my number, right?"

Micah's smile was sweet. "I do. Thank you for the number and for all of this. I have no doubt I'll get lost, but at least I have a vague idea of where I am."

Constantine wanted to stick around, but it wasn't his place. He stepped away, gesturing at the door. "You should knock."

Before he could, the door opened. Amyas looked at Micah, then at Constantine. "Good. Both of you are here. Mordred wants to see you."

Constantine blinked. "You mean he wants to see Micah."

"If that was what I meant, that's what I would have said. Mordred wants to see *both* of you."

Constantine had no idea why, but he wasn't going to argue. If Mordred needed him to do something, he'd say yes, and if it meant spending more time with Micah, that would be even better.

They both followed Amyas into the office. Mordred was sitting behind his desk, looking at something on his computer, but he smiled at them. He gestured at the chairs on the other side of his desk, and Constantine and Micah both settled down. Amyas was still there, and he took a seat on the arm of Mordred's chair. Mordred wrapped an arm around his waist.

It was good to see Mordred this way. He'd always been serious and quiet, but having Amyas in his life had changed him a bit. He smiled more often now, and he was obviously more relaxed. Amyas was a much needed and welcome addition to the household, even though some people grumbled about it since he was a supernatural creature.

It was odd to Constantine that Bowen had no problem accepting Amyas's presence, but he did when it came to Micah. Heroes were trained to distrust supernatural creatures and completely trust the conclave members, yet Bowen felt the opposite.

"Thank you for coming in," Mordred said with a smile.

"I'm not sure why I'm here," Constantine said.

"Because I'd like another point of view. You're one of the fallen heroes I trust the most."

Constantine leaned back in his chair, stunned. "I am?"

"You've always been present when I needed help, and you volunteer much more than anyone else to go on missions. I also like the way you took in Percy. Many fallen heroes weren't willing to give him a chance, and the same goes for Micah. You didn't let what they were and how Percy behaved stop you, though. I don't think we'd have managed to convince Percy to come to our side if it weren't for you."

Constantine snorted. "He came to our side because of Bay."

"I'm sure Bay is the main reason he decided to stay, but you offered him friendship when he didn't expect to get it. You kept who Micah was a secret, not even telling your best friend that Micah was working with us. I know it's created problems between you and Bowen."

Constantine didn't want to talk about his friend. "I'm just doing what I feel is right."

"Which is why I trust you. You don't have to be involved if you'd rather not be, though. I'll understand if you decide to leave."

Constantine wasn't going anywhere. Being here gave him a chance to be close to Micah, but he also wanted to make Mordred proud. He wanted the conclave to pay for what they'd done and how many people they'd hurt, and that wouldn't happen if he turned around and left. "I'm listening."

Mordred looked at Micah. "Do you trust him, too?"

"I trust your opinion of him. I don't know him well enough, but then, I don't know anyone well enough yet."

"Can we go over what happened yesterday once again?"

Micah leaned forward as he explained. Constantine had already heard this, but listening to it again made him realize how close Micah had been to being imprisoned or even killed. If he hadn't expected the other conclave members to corner him in his office, if he hadn't managed to run out as soon as he realized why they were there, he'd be in a cell right now, about to be put on trial.

And Constantine had no doubt that the trial would have ended in Micah's death. No one took those trials seriously. They were a way for the conclave to say they were doing things as they should when really, they weren't. They decided whether or not to execute people way before they were put on trial, and Constantine doubted anything would change their minds.

"I think I should contact Claire and Johnson," Micah said.

"After what happened with Marsha, you trust them to go along with what we're doing?" Mordred asked.

Constantine felt a bit out of place. He didn't want to make a nuisance of himself, and he learned a lot just by listening. He had many questions, though.

"I'm still convinced Verne did something to Claire to push her to side with him. She looked terrified, Mordred."

"Then wouldn't she be afraid to go against the rest of the conclave?"

"I have no doubt she will be, and it might take me a while

to convince her, but I truly believe she dislikes what the conclave has become. I wouldn't be surprised if she and Johnson wanted out, but as you know, that's not possible."

"Unless you're a traitor," Constantine piped in.

Micah smiled at him. "Unless you're a traitor, yes. But then, my punishment for that would have been death, which I suppose is the best way to get rid of a conclave member. I'll try contacting Claire and Johnson, and hopefully Kalliope will be on our side, too. We need more allies, though. The fallen heroes are strong, but there aren't enough of them."

Mordred tapped his fingertips on his desk. "We've been reaching out to the supernatural community. Most of the creatures are hesitant, though."

Amyas snorted loudly. "Can you blame them? For thousands of years, the conclave and the heroes have been after them. Why should they trust the fallen heroes?"

"I understand that it won't be easy for them to trust us, but I doubt we'll be able to take on the conclave and what remains of the heroes on our own," Micah said. "More importantly, I believe the community should be part of the next conclave."

That was the first time Constantine heard about this, and he was stunned. "You mean you want them to be heroes?"

"That wouldn't be possible, but I do think the supernatural community should be part of the conclave. I don't know how many species would need to sit on it, but it can't just be composed of heroes. We tried that once, and it didn't work. We should consider opening the conclave to the rest of the world. Heroes can only be born, but it doesn't mean they're the only ones who can defend humanity. I'm sure that some people in the supernatural community would like to defend and protect their people, too."

That wasn't something Constantine had ever thought of. To be honest, he hadn't thought about much beyond getting rid of the conclave and keeping the innocents safe from them.

That was why he wasn't the guy in charge. He couldn't think that far ahead, not when they had a big problem to solve first.

But he was excited. He liked what Micah was saying, and he wanted to see it happen. Micah was right when he said that having only heroes in the conclave hadn't worked.

They had to find a better way to deal with this, and Micah's solution might just be the best one.

CHAPTER SIX

M icah had been to thousands of meetings since he'd become a conclave member, but none of them had been as nerve-racking as the one he was about to attend.

He and Mordred had a plan, but it wouldn't be easy to put it in place. The heroes had hurt supernatural creatures time and time again over thousands of years, and they wouldn't forget that easily, if at all. Micah didn't need them to forget it, though. He just needed them to give him and the fallen heroes a chance, and he hoped that together, they could defeat the conclave and create something that would work for everyone.

To make that happen, he'd have to be convincing.

"Who are we meeting again?" he asked Mordred.

Luckily, Mordred seemed amused more than irritated at Micah's question. "Harpies. They're one of the most numerous groups in the supernatural community, so it would be great if we could get them on our side."

Micah nodded and peered at their little group. Well, it wasn't that little. Of course, there were he and Mordred, but also Amyas, Constantine, Haven, Dimitri, Thor, and Cecil. Micah hoped that having several supernatural creatures with them would show the harpies that they were truly trying to do the right thing, but there was no way to be sure.

They were meeting in a neutral place, so hopefully, the harpies would be relaxed, or at the very least, willing to listen.

They finally reached a spot that Mordred deemed deep enough in the forest to open a portal. Mordred created it, and he gestured at everyone to step through. Micah obeyed, sticking close to the group and, in particular, to Constantine.

Micah had only arrived at the fallen heroes' house a few days ago, but he and Constantine had been spending a lot of time together. Micah was busy between meetings with Mordred, phone calls, and video calls, but when he wasn't, Constantine was never far. They talked about everything, from when they'd been born to how they'd become heroes to what had happened to Constantine after he'd left. Micah enjoyed spending time with him, and he could see their friendship becoming more, but he was in no rush to make that happen. No matter how much he wanted to have a private life and happiness, first, he had to deal with the conclave. Until Verne and his friends were gone, no one would be truly safe.

Micah wasn't surprised to find out that the neutral space was a national park. Whatever human was around would be far enough away that they wouldn't see the harpies, which was what mattered. It would be a problem if anyone saw them, but then, Dimitri also would be a problem.

He was very *green*.

The harpies were already there, waiting for them. It had been a while since Micah had last seen one, but they hadn't changed. Their bodies were those of big birds of prey, while their faces were human. It was an odd mix, one that had always intimidated Micah.

The three harpies looked like each other. Their feathers were dark brown and gray, and if Micah had to guess, they were related. They also had a similar hair color.

Micah swallowed. After exchanging a glance with Mordred, he stepped forward. "Greetings. My name is Micah, and until a few days ago, I was a conclave member."

The harpies seemed to have already talked, because the one who stepped forward didn't hesitate. "My name is Cassandra."

Micah nodded and gestured at his friends. He introduced

them one by one, and he didn't miss the way Cassandra's gaze stopped on the supernatural creatures especially. She was obviously curious, and Micah would answer any question she had. He suspected she'd have more of them for the supernatural creatures than for him, though.

"These are Tempest and Liana," Cassandra said. "We got your message, and we came. What do you want from us?"

"As I'm sure you noticed, I said I was a conclave member until a few days ago. I'm not anymore."

"Why should I care?"

Cassandra wasn't making this easy, but then, Micah hadn't expected her to. "You should care because, for several decades, I've been helping the fallen heroes. I sent them information from the inside, which is one of the reasons they managed to stop so many conclave missions from happening, and through that, saved many supernatural creatures. The fallen heroes have been helping your community for a long time, and even if you don't trust them, you can't deny that."

Cassandra huffed. "Who said I didn't trust them?"

Micah shouldn't have assumed. "I apologize. You might trust them, but I know you don't trust me, and I don't blame you. You have nothing that proves I've been working with the fallen heroes except for my word."

"What do you want from us?"

That was the crucial point of Micah's speech. "We want to change things. The conclave hasn't worked well in hundreds of years, and no matter how hard I tried from the inside, I came to realize that wasn't possible. That means we have to take the conclave head-on and destroy them. And to do that, the fallen heroes will need help."

Cassandra and the other two exchanged a glance. Micah expected one of the other harpies to speak, but Cassandra did so again. "You want our help."

"Yes. I believe that the only way to destroy the conclave is to face them as a community. We need to gather as many fighters as we can."

"And what will happen once the conclave is destroyed? Will you become king?"

Micah was horrified by that suggestion. "I never wanted to be a conclave member, and I still don't. The only reason I did was that I thought I'd be able to change things and make it easier on the supernatural community. When I realized I couldn't, I reached out to Mordred. I have no intention of being in power ever again. After so many years, my only goal is to get rid of the conclave, set up a new one that includes supernatural creatures, and retire."

Cassandra cocked her head. "You want to create a conclave that will have supernatural creatures on it?"

"I believe that's the only way a conclave can work. The supernatural community, humanity at large, and even heroes, need protection. Not everyone knows how to fight, and they shouldn't have to. That means they need someone to protect them, and who better than their own people? As I see it, I think that every big community of supernatural creatures should have a seat on the conclave, and of course, that the hero ranks should be open."

"We can never be heroes."

"I don't think you should have to be a hero to protect your people. Of course, this is just an idea. There are many people to talk to and many things to think about before we can even start putting this in place, but I believe this would be the best outcome for everyone."

"I can't give you an answer right now."

Micah found himself smiling. It wasn't a no, which was all that mattered. "And I don't expect one. I realize you have to talk to your people, and I don't have a problem with that. But we should act as quickly as possible. Now that I ran away, the conclave members are angry and won't hesitate to strike.

They'll try to hurt me through the fallen heroes, and possibly the supernatural community."

And he didn't want that to happen. There had been enough pain and death. The last thing Micah wanted was to create more of it, but he knew he would. The only way to win this fight was to destroy the conclave, and that couldn't be done without shedding blood.

Constantine was fascinated by the passion in Micah's voice. Obviously, he meant what he was saying, and there was no way the harpies wouldn't trust him after this.

Okay, so maybe Constantine had a slight crush on the man. Who wouldn't? Micah was one of the bravest people Constantine had ever met. He'd put his life in danger for decades to help the fallen heroes and do what was right. Even now that he'd finally left the conclave and could have a better life, he was still fighting, and he wouldn't stop until the conclave finally did the right thing.

He was also gorgeous. Constantine wanted to lose himself in Micah's gray eyes, to run his fingers in his floppy hair. When they walked next to each other, his hands itched to grab him.

What would Micah do if Constantine did exactly that? He wasn't a conclave member anymore, so there was nothing that said they couldn't be together, but he'd just arrived at the house. He probably didn't know what he wanted to do next, and Constantine didn't want to push him into staying or anything like that. Many fallen heroes eventually got their own place, and they only came around when Mordred needed them. Constantine didn't want that to happen with Micah, but Micah deserved to get whatever he wanted after everything he'd done.

The harpies looked at each other. They had the kind of

conversation people who knew each other extremely well could have with their gazes, and Constantine held his breath. They weren't the ones who would be making decisions, but whatever they were about to say would show which way they were leaning. Would they trust Micah?

To Constantine's surprise, Liana stepped forward. Cassandra made a hissing sound and reached for her, but Liana shook her head and raised her chin high. "It's a pleasure to meet you, Micah, former conclave member," she said. "I am the leader of my tribe."

Constantine blinked. He hadn't expected that. And from the expression on the faces of some of the others who'd come with them, he wasn't the only one.

Micah didn't look surprised, though, and he bowed lightly, pressing his hand against his chest. "It's an honor to meet you."

"Did you mean everything you just said? Would you really have a conclave with a harpy on it?"

"I would," he confirmed.

Constantine released the breath he'd been holding. This was going the way they'd hoped it would.

"I can't say I ever expected to hear those words from anyone from the conclave, and I have doubts, but the harpies will help you. When the time comes, call us. We'll fight by your side." She paused. "But remember what you promised."

"I won't go back on that promise. Having a diverse conclave is the only way to make things work in the future. If we can't do this, humanity and the supernatural community will be in danger."

Liana nodded and opened her wings. Constantine watched in awe as she pushed into the air and flapped them, getting higher and higher. The other two harpies quickly nodded at Micah, then followed their leader. Constantine watched them for as long as he could, which wasn't very long considering they were in the middle of trees. Only once the harpies were out of sight did he turn back to Micah. "Did you know she was the leader?"

Micah shook his head. "I had no idea. I'm not surprised she wanted to hear what I had to say, though. It's what any leader would want. It also takes less time for her to be here than to have to wait for Cassandra to fly back to her, tell her what happened, then fly back to us."

"Well, that went well," Mordred said, clapping Micah's back. "I'm proud of you."

Constantine's eyes widened, but Micah didn't seem offended. If anything, he seemed proud of himself, and he was right to be. He'd done something Constantine hadn't thought was possible. He'd convinced harpies to work with the fallen heroes against the conclave.

There was a bounce in Constantine's step as they walked back to the spot where Mordred had opened the first portal. He opened a second one, and Constantine stuck close to Micah as all of them walked through.

"That was incredible," Constantine said as they headed toward the house.

Thankfully, Micah seemed amused rather than irritated by his enthusiasm. "It was. I didn't expect it to be so easy, to be honest."

Constantine snorted. "Now every other meeting will be complicated, and it'll be your fault."

Micah grinned. "I doubt I have that kind of power."

"You have a lot of power," Constantine murmured, staring at Micah so hard that he stumbled and almost fell on his face.

Thankfully, Micah was there. He grabbed Constantine's arm and pulled him close. Constantine didn't fall, and as a bonus, he got to be pressed against Micah's side for a bit. He looked up at Micah, grinning like an idiot, and was relieved and happy to see that Micah was smiling down at him.

"Will you be okay if I let you go?" Micah asked.

"I'm just excited about everything that's happening." Constantine straightened. "You know, I've been a fallen hero for a few decades, and I've been fighting the conclave since then. It almost felt as if there would be no end to this, but now, I know there will be. I can even see it, and while we have a huge fight in our future, at least we're finally moving forward."

Micah released Constantine's arm after squeezing it and started walking again. "I understand how you feel. The entire time I worked from inside the conclave, I wished I could do more. I wanted to end the conclave right away, but it wouldn't have been possible. Most days, it felt like what I was doing was useless."

"It wasn't useless. You saved many lives by giving us the information about the missions."

"I realize that. But I wanted to do more. I wanted to do something more concrete, and I finally am. It's terrifying, yet, at the same time, exciting."

They reached the house, and Constantine opened the door for Micah. A few heroes were hanging around the entrance, obviously waiting to find out what happened with the harpies. Constantine grinned at them and gave them a thumbs-up, and they broke into smiles. Constantine didn't miss the fact that Bowen was there, too, and like he always seemed to be, he was glaring at Micah.

Constantine stepped closer to Micah, just in case Bowen decided to do something stupid. Constantine hoped he wouldn't, but he was starting to realize he'd never truly known his friend.

The Bowen he'd known wouldn't have reacted this way to what Micah was doing. He would have wanted to help, and he would have been in awe of what was happening. Instead, Bowen was angry, and everyone was beginning to notice. It had started with Percy, but it was obvious Bowen had something against Micah, and Constantine didn't understand.

If Mordred, Constantine, most of the other fallen heroes, and the supernatural creatures who lived with them could trust Micah, why couldn't Bowen?

Constantine almost went to his old friend, but he decided to stay next to Micah instead. He didn't want to give Bowen an explanation. He didn't owe him one, anyway. He'd been on a mission, and they'd come back victorious. Instead of being happy about that, Bowen looked like he wanted to punch something, and Constantine would make sure it wasn't his face.

"Thank you for coming with us," Micah said as they walked away from the entrance.

Constantine wasn't sure where they were headed, but he started walking toward the library, since he knew the house. It was one of his favorite rooms, even though he didn't read much. But it was peaceful, and many fallen heroes preferred the living room or the kitchen. That meant the library was usually empty, which was perfect when Constantine needed time to himself.

"I'm glad Mordred asked me to go with you. I don't understand why he trusts me so much, but I'm glad he does," he told Micah.

Micah cocked his head. "How can you not understand? You've supported him every step of the way."

"As have many other fallen heroes. I'm not trying to get him to change his mind about me. I'm glad he trusts me with these missions." And that it meant he could spend time with Micah.

There was no way to know what would happen next, but whatever it was, it wouldn't be pretty. The conclave wouldn't go down without a fight. But this was what the fallen heroes had been training to achieve for the past few hundred years.

One way or another, the conclave would be destroyed.

Micah didn't want to be nosy, but he'd noticed Bowen glaring at him and Constantine. He wasn't surprised Bowen disliked him, but he didn't understand why the two friends were fighting.

"I saw Bowen earlier," he said as they reached what he thought was the library. He was glad to see he was right when Constantine pushed open the door and gestured him inside.

"I saw him, too," Constantine replied.

He flopped into one of the chairs under the window, and Micah took the one in front of him.

He looked around. He'd seen the library when Constantine had shown him around the house, but he hadn't taken time to come back yet. When would he have? He'd been busy in meetings with Mordred, getting to know the fallen heroes around the house, and going out to meet supernatural creatures. Well, that had only happened once, but it wouldn't be the last time. With the harpies on their side, Micah hoped other supernatural creatures would agree they could work together. That was what they needed to bring down the conclave, and every time a leader said *yes,* it was a step closer to getting what they needed

"I take it you're still fighting?" Micah asked as he continued looking around.

The library was gorgeous. Shelves covered every inch of the walls around him except for the window wall, each of them heavy with books. He wanted to check the title of every single one, find something to read, and lose himself in it for hours. He hadn't had the opportunity to do that since he was human, and he missed it.

He missed a lot of things from when he was human, and while he was never getting them back, it didn't mean that his new life was bad. He was glad he'd be able to change some things, though. Now that he wasn't with the conclave anymore, he'd be allowed to be himself and to make his own decisions.

Constantine tilted his head back to stare at the ceiling. "It's not as much fighting as ignoring each other. Well, I'm trying to ignore him. Every time I see him, he glares."

"I'm sorry I was the cause for that."

Constantine's head snapped up. "You weren't. The reason we're fighting is that Bowen is a dickhead. Don't think for one second it's your fault."

Micah found himself smiling. He liked Constantine's personality. It would have been easy to dump Micah and fix things with Bowen, but that wasn't what Constantine was doing. He was convinced of what he believed, and in this case, it was that Micah was a good person and didn't deserve to be pushed away.

"But you've been friends for a long time," he said.

"We were in the conclave together. We kind of lost touch for a while after we left, but when Mordred found us, we reunited."

"And how long ago was that?"

"A few decades. Mordred found Bowen first. Bowen agreed to work for the fallen heroes, and together, they reached out to me."

"So he brought you into the fallen heroes."

"I suppose he did. We became closer again when I arrived here, but I think a lot of that was that I didn't know anyone else. Having Bowen was reassuring, and we drifted a bit away after a while. We were still friends, and things didn't start getting bad until Percy got here." Constantine shook his head. "I still don't understand why Bowen was so angry when Percy and I became friends."

Micah remembered what Amyas had said about Bowen

being jealous. "Maybe he doesn't want to share his friend."

"Share his friend?" Constantine snorted. "What am I, a toy? I can have many friends. Besides, that doesn't sound right. Bowen might have been my closest friend, but he wasn't my only one. He didn't have anything to say when I became friends with Amyas or Cecil. That's what I don't understand."

Constantine leaned forward. His eyes were wide and glittering, and it would be so easy for Micah to lose himself into them.

"As heroes, we're trained to hate supernatural creatures, right?" Constantine asked.

Micah blinked, trying to put his thoughts in order and not look like he'd been staring at Constantine. "Right," he confirmed.

Constantine nodded once. "So shouldn't he have been angry when I became Amyas's friend? Instead, it happened when I became Percy's friend, but Percy was a hero. Shouldn't it be easier for Bowen to accept that I'm Percy's friend rather than Amyas's?"

Micah suspected that Amyas was right and that Bowen was jealous. The reason he hadn't said anything when Constantine had become friends with Amyas and Cecil was that both of them were already in a relationship with someone. But Percy was, too, which meant Micah was probably wrong. "Maybe something happened between him and Percy?"

Constantine shrugged and threw himself back into the chair. "Well, he wasn't happy when we captured Percy. I think he didn't like playing babysitter, as he called it. He had better things to do than to stand guard outside Percy's cell. In the beginning, he agreed when I told him I'd take most of his shifts, but when I started talking to Percy, he got angry, and that changed."

"When did Percy and Bay get together?"

"Sometime after that. Bay visited him to try to change his

mind, but it took him a while. Percy can be stubborn when he wants to, which honestly, is most of the time."

Micah chuckled, but he was thinking about what Constantine had just said.

When he and Percy had met, Percy wasn't with Bay yet. Bowen could have been jealous of him.

Could Bowen be in love with Constantine?

Micah looked at the man in front of him. It wasn't hard to fall in love with Constantine. He was a lovely person, and Micah really liked him. He could see it would be easy for him to fall for Constantine, so he could understand why that had happened to Bowen. He didn't know if that was true, but he wouldn't be surprised, and it would explain why Bowen had been so angry with Percy, and now, with Micah.

When Constantine decided to do something, he threw himself into it entirely. That was what he'd done with Micah, showing him around the house and taking him under his wing. That probably was what he'd done with Percy, too.

And Bowen was jealous.

Constantine got to his feet and stretched. Micah couldn't look away, especially when Constantine's t-shirt rode up, exposing his stomach. His mouth went dry, and he licked his lips. Constantine didn't seem to notice and grinned at Micah once he was done stretching. "What do you think? Do you want to take a walk around the lake?"

"I'd love to." Micah got up. He'd say yes to pretty much anything if it meant he could spend more time with Constantine, but he did enjoy walks, and the lake was beautiful.

The entire area was beautiful. He didn't know if he'd stay with the fallen heroes once all of this was over, but he was tempted.

Constantine bounced on the balls of his feet. "And once we're done walking, we can grab some lunch. Hopefully, someone will cook."

"I could cook something."

Constantine's eyes widened. "When did you learn to cook?"

"As a conclave member, I didn't have nearly as much to do as when I was a hero. There were a lot of meetings, but all of those were with conclave members. I met with some heroes, too, but I had plenty of free time."

"You'll have to teach me someday. I suck at cooking."

"How come?"

Constantine chuckled and rubbed the back of his neck. "I don't have the patience to wait for things to cook, so I usually just raise the temperature in the oven or things like that. That's how I managed to serve a roast that was burned on the outside and raw inside."

Micah laughed. He couldn't remember the last time he'd felt so free, like whatever happened, everything would be okay. But being with Constantine made him feel that way.

If both of them made it out of this alive, he wanted to see if things between them could turn from friendship to something deeper. Hell, he wasn't sure he wanted to wait that long. There was no way to know how long it would take for them to take down the conclave, but it wouldn't be quick. There were too many people to contact and talk with and too many things to put in place.

Maybe it was time for Micah to stop waiting. That was what he'd done as a conclave member, but he wasn't one anymore.

Constantine was excited to spend time with Micah away from everyone else. He didn't know what would happen, but he was ready for anything as he led Micah out of the house, jumping down the stairs two by two until he reached the last one. Once he did, he turned toward the lake, trying to see it as if he never had before like Micah was. Well, Micah had seen it, but only from the inside of the house.

They wouldn't be able to walk all around the lake. It was too big, and there wasn't enough space to walk in some places. As it was, they'd have to climb up and down rocks, and Constantine hoped Micah wouldn't mind. He loved this kind of walk, where he had to put in some effort. That meant he was alone, which he sorely needed sometimes with so many people living in the same house.

They stood there, just under the house, with the lake spread in front of them. Micah took a deep breath and looked around, his eyes wide.

"It's beautiful."

It really was. The water was dark, and Constantine could see a couple of birds of prey flying around in the distance. They nested on the other side of the lake, and it wasn't the first time he'd seen them. They were impressively big, and he watched Micah as the man followed the birds' progression in the sky.

"This is one of the reasons I decided to stay and live here," he explained. "It's too beautiful not to."

"But you have to share the house with many people."

Constantine shrugged. "I didn't have any privacy when I was a hero. At least here, my bedroom is a decent size, and no one is ordering me around."

"Not even Mordred?" Micah asked with a smile.

"He's always ordering someone around, but even when he has things for us to do, it's more like he asks. He never wants to send someone on a mission they can't deal with."

Micah nodded. "He'd be a great conclave member."

Constantine grinned. "Can I be there when you suggest that? Please?"

Micah laughed. "He wouldn't be happy, would he?"

"I agree that he'd be a great conclave member, but I'm

pretty sure that once all of this is over, he wants to take some time to rest. He and Amyas didn't meet that long ago, and they deserve to spend time together."

"I agree."

"You could become a conclave member again," Constantine suggested as he turned around and started walking away from the house.

He heard Micah follow him, his steps more careful because he wasn't used to walking on these stones.

"I have no intention of ever sitting on the conclave again," Micah said. "I never wanted to be a conclave member to begin with. The only reason I did was that I wanted to keep an eye on the conclave members and try to change things. No matter how hard I tried, though, nothing changed, and here we are."

"Do you feel like you wasted time working with the conclave?"

"I don't. I might not like the time I spent there, but I wouldn't have been able to do everything I did if I'd left. I might have hated it, but it was useful."

"You're out now."

"I am. It's odd, to be honest. There's still a lot of work to do, but I also feel like I don't know what to do with my life. There are so many possibilities, especially once the conclave is dealt with. I don't know where to start."

"You don't have to decide now."

"I don't think I should decide now. There's no way to know what's going to happen once this gets serious."

What Micah wasn't saying was that there was a chance one or both of them would be dead by the time this was over.

But Constantine didn't want to think about that. He couldn't, not when he wouldn't back down from this fight. This was what he'd worked toward all these years, and even if he died, he'd know he died doing the right thing.

He still hoped he wouldn't die.

He and Micah walked around the lake for a bit. Every time Constantine peeked at Micah, it was to see the other man looking around. His expression was more relaxed than Constantine had ever seen it, and he liked that it was thanks to him that Micah felt okay. Micah needed time away from everything, and Constantine was the one who provided that.

He wanted to provide more, but he didn't know where to start or even if he should. He and Micah had a fight ahead of themselves, and they might not make it out alive. Was it a smart idea to start something now?

But Constantine would be hurt by Micah's death whether or not they were together. He couldn't stop his feelings, and he didn't want to. Instead, he wanted to see where things could go between them. Even if one of them didn't make it in the end, at least they'd have something.

Eventually, they stopped walking. They could see the house, but they were so far away that he doubted anyone from inside would see them. That was fine, because that way no one would notice Constantine moving closer, so close that if he wanted, he could have reached out and touched Micah.

And he wanted to. He just wasn't sure the gesture would be welcome.

Micah took a deep breath, then released it. He turned toward Constantine, and he didn't seem surprised to see Constantine so close. Instead, it made him smile and inch even closer.

"Thank you for this. I needed it," he said.

Constantine swallowed. "You're welcome. Anytime you want to take a walk, you just have to let me know, and I'll come with you."

"That's good to know." Micah's voice was getting softer. "Why are you doing this, though?"

"What? Going on walks with you?"

"Yes. You've never doubted that I was on your side. You

never hesitated to make me feel welcome."

"I don't know. Maybe it's because I knew what you were doing. Mordred told a few other people, including me. Or maybe it's just because I like the kind of person you are. It would have been so easy for you to ignore everything, keep your head down, and enjoy being a conclave member without trying to change anything. That's what the others are doing, after all."

"But I didn't," Micah whispered.

He leaned forward, and Constantine knew they were about to kiss. His heart raced as he moved closer, too, so close that their arms and chests brushed together. "You didn't," he confirmed. "You did something not many people would have done. You stood up for what you thought was right, and you worked to make it happen. I don't need to have been there to know it wasn't easy. I'm glad you made it out and to have the opportunity to fight by your side when the time comes."

"But we're not fighting yet."

"Not yet," Constantine murmured. He could feel Micah's breath on his skin. Neither of them was leaning closer, though. They were suspended in time, their lips barely brushing against each other, their breaths mingling. Micah's body was warm, and Constantine wanted to sink into him.

"And what will we do in the meantime?" Micah asked.

Constantine didn't answer with words. Instead, he finally pressed closer. Their lips touched, and Micah sighed against Constantine's mouth. He seemed to slump against Constantine, and Constantine was more than happy to hold him up.

He wrapped his arms around Micah. Micah had been strong until now, and he hadn't had anyone to support him. Constantine wanted that to change, and he wanted to be the person who'd support Micah when he needed it and even when he didn't. He wanted to be there for Micah the way Micah had been for the supernatural community.

Micah had been alone, and it was time for him not to be anymore.

Their first kiss was slow and gentle. Even though Constantine wanted nothing more than to drag Micah to his bed, there was no rush. They didn't need to go that quickly, though. Constantine wanted to believe they had all the time in the world to get to know each other and build their relationship. Even if they didn't, they weren't going to attack the conclave tomorrow, so they had a little time.

He had every intention of taking full advantage of that.

CHAPTER SEVEN

Word was going around that the fallen heroes were talking to the supernatural creatures' community. And to Micah's surprise, several groups had reached out. They wanted to talk to him and Mordred. And while he was stunned that they were so open, he was also eager to explain what his plans were for the future.

He'd never be a conclave member again. He didn't want to after the hundreds of years he'd been one. Once all of this was over and the new conclave was in place, he'd be taking a years-long vacation. He wanted to explore the world, and he hoped he wouldn't be alone.

Micah touched his lips. He should have been focused on the notes Mordred had taken while he'd been on the phone call with the leader of a naiad tribe Micah hadn't been present for, but instead, he couldn't stop thinking about Constantine and the kiss they'd shared by the lake. He hadn't expected it to happen, but he was glad it had. He wanted more kisses, and even more importantly, more Constantine.

They'd only met recently, but Micah couldn't imagine his life without Constantine in it anymore.

Constantine was by Micah's side from the moment he woke up to the moment he went to bed. It wasn't always physically. They spent as much time together as they could, considering what they both had to do, but even when Constantine wasn't there, Micah couldn't stop thinking about him.

Could they do this? With everything that was happening

and everything they had to do, could they really take the time to start a relationship and spend time together?

The answer should be no. Micah and the others should be focused on taking down the conclave, but Micah would never ask Mordred to stop spending time with Amyas so he could focus even more on this. He wouldn't ask it of anyone, and no one would ask it of him, either. If he wanted to explore a relationship with Constantine, no one would try to stop him except himself, and he didn't want to. For once, he wanted to be selfish and take something that was just for him.

Micah tapped his fingertips on the desk. He didn't have his own office the way Mordred did, and while Mordred had offered to share his with him, Micah would rather work on his own. Luckily, there was a desk in his room, so that was where he spent most of his days when they weren't out meeting with leaders and setting things up for the new conclave. The room was as private as an office would be, which meant no one would hear Micah's conversations.

And he needed to have at least two of them. Now that the supernatural communities in the country would back him against the conclave, he felt it was time to contact Johnson and Claire.

They might hang up on him and tell him they never wanted to hear from him again. They might tell him he was a traitor and threaten him the way Verne and his friends would if they ever saw Micah again. But Micah had to believe they'd do the right thing like he had. They hadn't before, but he understood why. They'd been afraid to lose everything, and if they agreed to help, they would. They wouldn't be conclave members anymore once the new conclave was in place.

But they'd be doing the right thing.

Micah swallowed and pulled the phone on the desk closer. Mordred had assured him that anyone he called through this phone wouldn't be able to use the call to find him thanks to a mix of technology and Cecil's magic, and Micah hoped it would work. He didn't want to lead the conclave to Mordred's doorstep.

He breathed in and out for a moment, trying to calm himself. There would be bloodshed in the fight to take down the conclave, but how much blood would depend on what happened next. Micah hoped he'd be able to convince Johnson, Claire, and Kalliope to put the other three conclave members on trial. They needed a majority, and with Micah, they would have it. If they managed to do that, Verne and his friends would finally get what they should have gotten a long time ago, and it would show the supernatural community that they were finally ready to do the right thing.

Then, once they decided what fate Verne and the others would meet, they could disband what remained of the conclave or maybe pull in members of the supernatural communities that their people would choose to replace the old members. Micah wasn't quite sure yet, but then, he supposed he didn't need to be. It would be a while before any of this could happen, and it still might never happen. It depended on whether or not Micah was convincing, and it was a heavy weight to have on his shoulders.

But he was the only one who could do this, and he'd do his best.

He picked up the phone and dialed Johnson's number. If there was one conclave member Micah was almost sure would go along with this, it was Johnson.

It took a while for the man to answer. When he did, he sounded wary. "Who is this?"

Micah sucked in a breath. "Hello, Johnson."

There was a pause before Johnson asked, "Micah?"

"It's me."

"What's going on? Why are you calling me?"

"Because we need to talk."

"What did you do? Verne's been going around telling everyone you're a traitor, and he wants to put you on trial. He's trying to convince Kalliope, Claire, and me to vote to have you executed."

Micah wasn't surprised. "And no one has said yes yet?"

"No. We have no idea what's going on."

"Well, I *am* a traitor," Micah confirmed.

"What are you talking about? What did you do?"

"Are you alone?"

"Yes. Just tell me, Micah."

Micah leaned back in his chair. "I've been working with the fallen heroes for a while. I've been giving them information on missions and heroes."

"Why would you do that?"

It was good that Johnson wasn't hanging up or running to get Verne. It meant he was willing to listen to Micah, which was all Micah needed. "Because what the conclave has been doing isn't right. We were created to protect humanity and the innocent. Why has that become a full-on war with the supernatural community? Why has the conclave been giving orders to kill children? You know that's what's happening, and you know it's wrong."

Micah wished he could see Johnson right now. He'd learned a while ago to read the expressions of the other conclave members because it was the only way to truly understand what went on in their minds most of the time. Johnson wasn't saying anything, and the silence was heavy, so much that Micah started wondering if he should hang up.

"You're right," Johnson eventually said.

Micah's shoulders slumped in relief. "You know that what Verne and the others are doing is wrong. We shouldn't be killing children, and especially not for what they are. They can't change the fact that they're supernatural creatures. They were born that way, and they shouldn't die just because of that."

110

"What do you want me to do?"

Micah wasn't about to give Johnson any details. It sounded like Johnson was on his side, but Micah couldn't be sure. He wasn't going to risk it. "I need to talk to Claire and Kalliope and to convince them and you to work with us."

"You want to turn us into traitors."

"I want the conclave to go back to what it was supposed to be. I want the conclave and heroes to be protectors, not mindless killers. That's not going to happen until we take care of Verne, Hester, and Elmer." Micah softened his voice. "I know you don't want to lose your spot as a conclave member. It's comfortable, and it keeps you safe. You have to realize that this can't go on, though."

"I'll talk to Claire," Johnson promised. "We'll talk to you in a few hours at the most."

"What about Kalliope?"

"I can't help you there. She hasn't been around lately, and I'm not about to try looking for her. If you need to talk to her, you're going to have to do it yourself."

That was much more than Micah had expected, so he wouldn't mind looking for Kalliope. First, though, he'd talk to Johnson and Claire, and hopefully, by the time the call was over, the fallen heroes would have two more conclave members on their side.

Constantine was smiling like an idiot, but he couldn't help it. Everything was going just right, including his new relationship with Micah. He had to focus on the video call he was on, though, so he pushed those thoughts away and looked at the two heroes on his screen. "Do you have any more questions?"

The two heroes looked at each other. They'd only recently left the conclave, and they were still wary. That was what the video call was for. Constantine had reassured them that they'd done the right thing by leaving the conclave and that they didn't have to fight against them they didn't want to. He hoped they'd become fallen heroes, but he wouldn't push them for something they weren't ready to give.

"How are the fallen heroes different from the conclave?" the woman asked. "There has to be a leader, right?"

"There is. Mordred was a hero, and he's a great person. I realize you don't know him and that you're wary, but we've been working hard to keep both humans and supernatural creatures safe. Unfortunately, sometimes, that meant killing heroes, or at the very least, fighting them. It makes us sound like the bad guys, but you know the conclave, maybe better than me since you were working with them until recently. What they're doing isn't right."

"But how do we know the fallen heroes won't be worse?"

Constantine leaned forward. "You can't know for sure, but Mordred has never asked me to kill children. That's why I left the conclave, you know? They asked me to kill a bunch of kids and their mothers, and I couldn't."

"When do you need our answer?" the man asked.

Constantine wished he remembered their names. He looked at the desk, trying to find the piece of paper where he'd written them down, but he couldn't. He supposed it wouldn't matter if they decided to retire and disappear, and if they didn't, well, he'd have time to get to know them.

"As soon as possible," he answered. "I know it's not an easy decision to make, but we won't stand back for much longer. We can't, not when the conclave is giving worse orders every day."

Micah wasn't with the conclave anymore, but that wasn't the only way they found out about the conclave's orders. An entire tribe of undines had been slaughtered just yesterday. There was not one tribe member alive, and thinking about it made Constantine want to go out there, find the conclave member who'd given that order, and kill them.

"We'll talk, and we'll let you know," the woman promised.

There wasn't much else to say after that, and when they hung up, Constantine leaned back in his chair and briefly closed his eyes. He thought he'd convinced them, but even if he hadn't, at least they weren't working for the conclave anymore. That was two heroes the fallen heroes wouldn't have to fight when the time came, and in the end, that was all that mattered.

Since the meeting was over, he got to his feet and headed out. He wanted to find Micah and spend time with him if he was available. From what Constantine knew, Micah had his own meetings, so maybe he'd enjoy taking another walk around the lake. It would be a good way to stretch their legs and spend time together.

He was almost at Micah's room when he noticed someone coming from the other side of the hallway. He groaned when he realized it was Bowen and briefly considered turning around, but he was pretty sure Bowen had seen him, and he didn't want to act as if he was afraid of his friends.

He wasn't. He just didn't want to talk to Bowen and have to listen to him spout bullshit about Micah and Percy. Constantine hoped Bowen would let him pass without stopping him, but of course, he was wrong. That would have been too easy.

"Constantine. I need to talk to you."

"Do we have to do this now? Because I have something to do."

Bowen's expression shifted to displeasure. "You never have time for me anymore. Every time I see you, you're either with that conclave member or Percy."

Constantine crossed his arms over his chest. "Maybe it's because of how angry you've become."

Bowen opened his mouth, then closed it and nodded. "I

know. I realize I haven't been behaving in the best of ways. Please, can we talk?"

Constantine didn't want to spend any length of time alone in a room with Bowen, but he felt he owed his friend at least that. He didn't think they'd ever be close again, but the least he could do was listen to what Bowen had to say. "Fine. But I don't have long."

"I don't need long."

Bowen opened the door of one of the guestrooms in the hallway, glanced around, and gestured at Constantine to follow him inside. It was empty, and it didn't look like it had been used recently, so Constantine doubted anyone would interrupt them, which was probably what Bowen had been aiming for.

Bowen closed the door behind Constantine and stepped closer. "What are you doing with him?" he asked.

Constantine scowled. "I thought you wanted to talk, not complain about Micah."

"I do want to talk, but I don't understand. He's a conclave member."

"He *was* a conclave member, and he's been working with us for longer than you and I have been fallen heroes. Why shouldn't I spend time with him and trust him?"

"He's not right for you."

Constantine blinked. "I'm sorry?"

"You think I didn't see you by the lake? I know he kissed you."

"We kissed, yes. How is that any of your business?"

"Don't you see? I should have told you sooner, but I was afraid you'd reject me. I'm not afraid anymore. I know we're perfect for each other."

Constantine opened his mouth to ask what the fuck Bowen was talking about, but he couldn't get one word out before Bowen's tongue was in his mouth.

Constantine spluttered and pushed Bowen away. Thankfully, Bowen had been focused on the kiss, so he didn't resist. He stumbled back, his eyes wide as Constantine wiped his mouth with his sleeve.

"What the fuck?" Constantine asked.

"Sorry. I shouldn't have surprised you."

"Damn right, you shouldn't have. Why did you kiss me?"

"Because I'm finally over my fear. We can be together now."

Constantine couldn't understand this. He and Bowen had only ever been friends. There had never been anything else between them, and there never would be because Constantine didn't feel that way. "Micah and I are dating," he said, even though he wasn't sure that was what they were doing.

"You can tell him it's over."

"I'm not going to do that, because there's nothing between us, Bowen. I've only ever seen you as a friend."

Bowen's expression turned angry. "How can you say that? We've been there for each other since we became heroes. You're my best friend."

"Exactly. I'm your *friend*, nothing more. I'm sorry, but I've never seen you in any other way, and I don't feel that way toward you."

Constantine doubted they'd remain friends. He wasn't even sure he wanted to. At least that explained why Bowen's behavior had been so erratic lately.

"You wouldn't feel like this if that damn conclave member hadn't arrived," Bowen snapped.

"I would, too. I've never seen you as anything more than a friend, Bowen. I'm sorry there can be nothing between us, but there wouldn't be even if Micah weren't in my life. It doesn't mean we can't be friends."

Bowen snorted. "Not as long as you're spending time with traitors."

Constantine didn't have to ask to know who he was talking about. As far as Bowen was concerned, both Percy and Micah were traitors. It didn't make sense, but then nothing did right now. "Then I'm sorry, but we can't be friends anymore. I won't abandon Percy and Micah because you can't admit they're on our side."

"You'll regret this," Bowen threatened.

Constantine doubted Bowen would do anything to him, but the threat still made him uneasy. There was nothing more he could say. Bowen was stubborn, and he'd already made his decision. He wouldn't trust Percy and Micah, and now that Constantine had rejected him, he wouldn't trust him, either.

When Johnson called back, it was a video call. Micah wasn't surprised, and he made sure there was nothing in the room that could identify the house before answering. Thankfully, the desk faced the window rather than having its back to it, so Johnson wouldn't see outside. He'd see the furniture, but there was no way for him to know where the house was.

Micah clicked and accepted the call. He was surprised to see Johnson wasn't alone. Claire was sitting next to him, and she leaned forward when Micah appeared on the screen, maybe to see if he was okay.

"I thought for sure Johnson was lying to me," she said.

Micah found himself smiling. "I doubt he'd have lied about something this big."

Claire shook her head. "It just doesn't make sense. Why did you contact Johnson?"

"Hasn't he told you?"

"He has, and I think this is nuts. You can't really be thinking about overthrowing the conclave."

Micah had expected her to be wary and hesitant, and he

was ready for it. "I am. I don't see what other option there is after everything they've done."

"You were a conclave member until recently, too, and Johnson and I still are."

"But the conclave works on a majority. Verne, Elmer, and Hester already have three votes. They only need a fourth to get whatever they want."

Claire looked right at Micah. "And when it comes to Marsha, they had my vote."

"I'm still wondering why you went along with it, to be honest. It wasn't like you."

Claire sighed and leaned back in her chair. "It wasn't." She hesitated and looked at Johnson. "But Verne found out something about me, and he's using it to blackmail me."

Micah wasn't surprised he'd been right or that Verne was blackmailing Claire. "You don't have to tell me. I don't need to know what's going on, just that you're on my side."

"We've talked about it," Johnson intervened. "You won't tell us your plans, will you?"

"I can't, and you won't be involved until everything is in place. Once it is, I need you to stand by my side and demand a trial for Verne, Elmer, and Hester."

"You'll need a fourth vote."

"I'm hoping that once I convince you to be on the right side of things, I'll be able to do the same thing with Kalliope. Contacting her is harder, though."

"And you really think you can do this?"

"As long as we have the majority, we'll be able to call for a trial. I know I'm not the only one who feels like the conclave has lost its way. Since I arrived here, I've talked to many fallen heroes, and all of them had a similar story to tell me. They left the conclave because they were given orders they couldn't follow, like killing children and innocent people. That's not what the conclave is about. We should be protecting the innocent, whether human or supernatural. Instead, we're killing children."

"Verne and the others are pushing to elect a new conclave member," Claire said.

Micah huffed. "I have no doubt it would be someone on their side so they have the majority."

"Johnson and I have been stalling for time, but we won't be able to do that forever, and once another conclave member is elected, you won't have any power anymore. If you want to do this, you have to be fast."

That was worrying. Micah wasn't sure they had everything in place to win this fight. Claire was right, though. If he wanted to put Verne and the others on trial, he had to be a conclave member. If another one was elected, he'd lose his power, and he wouldn't be able to do anything about it.

He had to make a decision. Did he trust them to know what he and fallen heroes were planning, or would he rather keep them in the dark? He needed them to continue stalling over this new conclave member.

"How long do I have?" he asked.

Claire and Johnson looked at each other again. "A few weeks, maybe three, if Kalliope doesn't come back," Johnson answered. "They need the rest of the conclave members to vote on this new member, and I have no doubt that Verne will blackmail both Claire and me with what he knows. We might not have a choice in voting for whoever he wants to take your place."

"I'll talk with my friends, and hopefully we'll be able to intervene soon."

"We'll do what we can."

"Are you on our side, then?" Micah had to know. Johnson and Claire seemed to understand what he was talking about, and there was no way for him to be a hundred percent sure they were on his side, but he had to trust them.

"What will happen to us once Verne and the others are put on trial?" Claire asked.

"The conclave will be disbanded. A new one needs to be built from the ground up, and we can't be part of it."

Micah thought for sure that would be a dealbreaker, so he was surprised when Claire smiled. "So Johnson and I will be free to go?"

"You will."

"We're with you, then. It's time to get rid of this conclave, and I personally want nothing to do with whatever happens next."

Micah had expected he'd have to work to convince her to step away from the conclave. He wanted to ask why she wasn't fighting for her seat, but he suspected it had to do with whatever Verne was blackmailing her with. He was curious, but it was none of his business, so he didn't ask what it was.

"Do you have any idea where Kalliope is?"

Johnson shook his head. "She's disappeared. She was gone even before you, and Verne is pissed because he can't hold a vote on his new conclave member until she's found. You need to find her before he does."

"I have a few ideas." And Micah hoped he'd find her where he conjectured.

Kalliope was never easy to deal with, and most of the time, Micah didn't understand which way she would go until she opened her mouth. He had to convince her to side with them, and that meant finding her before Verne did.

"We won't stand in your way, and we'll help as much as we can considering our position, but I hope you don't expect us to publicly stand up to Verne until you're ready to put everything in place," Johnson said.

"I never expected you to take the same risk I took. All I need is your assurance that when I stand up to Verne and put him and the others on trial, you'll be by my side and vote with me." And once that was done, they'd have to bow out of the conclave and allow the new one to step in.

"We will," Claire promised.

Micah could only pray she and Johnson wouldn't change their minds. He knew Verne, so he wouldn't be surprised if the man found a way to get to them. But if they wanted to be free, this was the only way to make that happen.

There was nothing else Micah could do. He'd spoken his mind, and they'd agreed to help him. The next step would be to convince Kalliope to side with them, then once she said yes, to attack the conclave building and get to Verne, Elmer, and Hester. With the backing of another three conclave members, Micah would put them on trial, and they'd find the three guilty of trying to get rid of the supernatural community using heroes. They'd be executed, and the new conclave could be put into place.

Thinking about it, it sounded easy. Micah knew it would be anything but. Convincing Kalliope would be complicated, and even once she was on their side, they'd have to get into the conclave building and reach Verne and his friends. That meant they'd have to fight heroes who still worked for the conclave, and he wasn't looking forward to that.

Heroes were a family, or at least, they used to be. The conclave had perverted that, and Micah hoped that it would go back to what it was supposed to be in time. In the meantime, they couldn't allow anyone to stop them, not even other heroes.

That meant they'd have to fight and spill each other's blood.

Constantine had been looking for Micah, but after his conversation with Bowen, he didn't want to upset him. He was upset enough himself, and he needed to find a way to deal with his emotions and wrap his mind around them, so he headed to the gym.

It wasn't that he liked training. Really, who would enjoy getting sweaty and tired? But ever since he'd become a hero, he'd been forced into training every day, and that hadn't changed after he'd left the conclave. If he wanted to protect people, he needed to be strong, which was why he was ready to run on the treadmill or lift weights. Hopefully, the pain in his muscles would be enough to eclipse the pain in his heart over losing a friend.

But when he got to the gym, he found Percy was already there. He hadn't expected to be alone, because all the fallen heroes used the gym, but he didn't think he could lie to Percy. They were friends, and they were close enough that Constantine could tell when something was on Percy's mind. He had no doubt the same went for Percy, even though he was gruffer about it.

Percy disliked showing anyone he was vulnerable. He was wary of opening himself up to people, and Constantine was humbled that he was one of the few Percy viewed as a friend. That was one of the reasons he had opposed Bowen over this. He couldn't betray Percy's trust.

Percy looked up when the door creaked, and he smiled at Constantine. His blond hair was tied on top of his head, and his cheeks were flushed. He was sweating, so Constantine kept his distance.

"Something happened," Percy said after a moment.

"Don't worry about it."

But Percy shook his head and got up from the machine he'd been using. He grabbed a towel hanging on it, wiped his face and arms, and stepped closer. "How can I not worry? You're one of my closest friends, and I don't want anything to happen to you. You don't have to talk about it if you don't want to, but I'd like to know what's going on."

Constantine flopped onto one of the benches that lined the walls. He buried his face in his hands, his mind going back to the conversation he had with Bowen.

"Bowen cornered me," he eventually admitted.

Percy swore. "Did he hurt you? Because if he did, I'm going to kick his ass."

"He didn't touch me, or at least, not in the way you're thinking."

There was a moment of silence before Percy asked. "What does that mean?"

Constantine realized how it sounded and looked at his friend. "Just that he tried to kiss me. That's all there was to it, though."

Percy sat next to Constantine. "Do you need me to kick his ass?"

"If I wanted someone to kick his ass, I could have done so myself. No, to be honest, I don't want anything to do with him anymore."

"And you're sad because you lost a friend."

"I just don't understand what happened. I never did anything that could make him think I was interested in having a relationship with him. He's always only been a friend, and I never thought about him as anything else."

"But he did."

Constantine groaned. "He did, and I think he's been jealous of you and Micah. He keeps insisting he doesn't like you because you're traitors, but I know that's not the case after what he tried to do today."

"I'm sorry." And he sounded like he really was, even though none of this was his fault.

"Don't worry about it. You had nothing to do with this. Bowen did everything on his own, and all of this is his fault, no one else's. I'm sorry I lost a friend, but I'm also relieved at this point. Even after I pushed him away, he insisted we should be together. He couldn't understand that I didn't see him that way, and he thought that the only reason I was saying no was Micah."

Constantine hesitated. He hadn't thought anyone would see them when they'd kissed by the lake, but Bowen had. Did that mean he was spying on them? A few days ago, Constantine would have said that wasn't possible, but now, he wondered.

He and Micah hadn't talked about telling anyone that they were seeing each other, but Percy was Constantine's best friend. He was telling him about Bowen, and it would be easier for him to understand the situation if he was aware that Constantine and Micah were together.

Of course, Constantine wasn't a hundred percent sure they were. They'd kissed by the lake, and they'd walked back to the house holding hands, but they hadn't talked yet. Every time they saw each other, they found themselves making out or having to act normally because they were in the presence of other people.

"There's something else," Percy said.

"Just that Bowen saw Micah and me kiss."

"I suppose that explains why Bowen is so angry with Micah."

"I doubt it has anything to do with Micah being an ex-conclave member. Now that I know he's in love with me, it's obvious it's jealousy."

"You think he'll try to use what he saw against you and Micah?"

Constantine shrugged. "I don't see how he could. I mean, even if he tells Mordred he saw us kissing, what will that do? I doubt Mordred will care. He's known Micah for a long time, and he trusts him entirely. If anything, I suspect he'd be happy to know that Micah has someone in his life."

Percy patted Constantine's knee. "Then I wouldn't worry.

I'm sorry you lost a friend, but it sounds like Bowen did everything on his own. You were honest with him, and you can't do anything about the fact that he can't accept it."

"I know." But Constantine was worried. Something was about to happen, but he didn't know if it had to do with the conclave or with Bowen. Hopefully, even though they'd fought, Bowen still believed in the fallen heroes' mission.

The gym door opened, and Bay stepped in. His eyebrows rose high on his forehead when he saw the position Constantine and Percy were in. Percy still had a hand on Constantine's knee, but he didn't act guilty because there was nothing for them to be guilty about. He gave one last squeeze, then he got up to greet his boyfriend.

"Should I be jealous?" Bay teased.

Constantine groaned. "Please, not you, too."

Bay blinked in surprise. "Who else is jealous?"

"Bowen," Percy answered. "Apparently, that's why he doesn't like me. He thought Constantine and I would get together."

"But he knows you won't."

"And now, he's jealous of Micah," Constantine said.

"Does he have a reason to be jealous of Micah?"

Constantine supposed he might as well tell Bay. He doubted Percy would tell his boyfriend, but Constantine didn't have a reason to keep this a secret. Hopefully, Micah would agree. "We've been spending some time together, and we kissed. For now, that's all there is to it."

"It's good, though."

Constantine smiled. "You really think so?" This was the kind of support he'd needed from Bowen, but instead, he was getting it from Bay and Percy. As sad as he was to lose a friend, he couldn't say he'd be losing a lot.

"Micah needs this, I think. He's been working in the dark for a long time, and as he did so, he had to ignore his personal life. It would have been too dangerous for him to have anyone in his life. Now, he's free, yet at the same time, he's not. We have a huge fight in front of us, and if something happens to him during that fight, he'll have wasted decades of his personal life. It's a sacrifice he's willing to make, but I don't see the problem if it means he can have a little happiness before anything else happens. Besides, I think the two of you are good for each other."

Constantine hoped so, but he and Micah were barely together.

"You are," Percy confirmed. "So don't listen to what Bowen told you or what other people will say. You're one of the few here who knows Micah, and I think you should trust your instincts when it comes to him."

Constantine had every intention of doing so, but he was relieved that he'd have support if anything happened. Bay and Percy didn't have a problem with him and Micah being together, and neither would Mordred. The only one who did was Bowen, and it had nothing to do with trusting Micah and everything to do with jealousy.

Constantine could deal with that. He could deal with a lot of things if it meant being with Micah.

CHAPTER EIGHT

It was time for the next step of Micah's plan.

He was nervous, but he had to talk to Kalliope. He knew where to find her, and he had to make his move before she left. Hopefully, she'd listen to him and side with him, but there was no way for him to know for sure, and it made him nervous. Claire and Johnson had been the easy part of this plan. Kalliope would be a tough one, and Micah couldn't say he was looking forward to the conversation they were about to have.

"Are you sure you don't want anyone else to go with you?" Mordred asked.

Micah and Constantine looked at each other. Constantine was the only person who would be going with Micah. He'd be able to protect Micah if anything happened, but a group of two would feel less like they were trying to intimidate Kalliope into siding with them.

That was what Micah hoped, anyway.

"The two of us will be fine," he told Mordred. "But we'll have our phones if anything happens. We'll let you know."

"I still don't like this. She might try to have you arrested."

"She might, but she has no way to know I'm coming. I won't have long, not if she decides to throw me to the wolves, but if I can convince her to listen to me, I'll be fine."

"And if you can't convince her?"

"Then I'll get him out of there," Constantine promised. "You have to trust me to keep him safe."

Mordred looked from Constantine to Micah, then nodded

curtly. "I do trust you, Constantine. And I trust Micah to do this. I just don't want to lose either of you. The conclave has already taken so many people from us."

Micah's chest felt tight. He'd lost many heroes he considered friends over the decades. He'd had to keep his distance from them when he'd become a conclave member, but he'd always kept an eye on them. Some had left the conclave, while others had been killed, usually on missions. He wouldn't allow the conclave to take anyone else from him, especially not Constantine.

"I'll call you as soon as we're done with Kalliope," he promised. "If you don't hear from me in fifteen minutes, you can send the cavalry."

Mordred pointed a finger at him. "I'll hold you to that."

"I wouldn't expect anything different from you."

Mordred took a step back, and Constantine looked at Micah. He'd be the one to open the untraceable portal to reach Kalliope. That way, Constantine wouldn't have to control the portal and would be able to focus on their safety.

Constantine was armed to the teeth, both with guns and blades. Micah had never been attracted to weapons, but he had to admit they looked good on Constantine. To be honest, it was probably overkill, but if it made Constantine feel better about protecting Micah, Micah wasn't about to protest.

He held his hand out and created the portal. He and Constantine looked back at Mordred one last time, then stepped through. Constantine went first, and Micah waited for him to give him the okay to follow him.

He wrinkled his nose at the sight that greeted him. He wasn't surprised that this was where Kalliope holed up when she spent time away from the conclave. She was ancient, but still. Making an ancient temple her home?

Micah wasn't sure what this place had been, but the temple was gorgeous. Columns stood in front of him, framed by old olive trees. Most of the temple seemed to be still standing, although it now opened on the empty sky. There were more ruins, bits of walls he could still see the outline of, and he wanted to explore, but that wasn't why he was here.

There were more columns beyond the one he could see in front of him, maybe another temple? He'd have to ask Kalliope.

"This place is incredible," Constantine murmured.

"It is," Micah agreed. If they hadn't been here for Kalliope, this would have been a perfect spot for a first date.

He eyed Constantine. They hadn't had the time to talk, let alone go on a date, but he wanted to do that. There was no way to know if they'd make it out of the fight that was waiting for them alive, and he didn't want to miss even one experience with Constantine.

But now wasn't the time to think about that. Now was the time to focus on Kalliope. And as if Micah had called her through his thoughts, he looked up to see her walking between the columns, coming toward them.

She wore a flowing red dress, and her black hair was loose and framed her face. It was very dramatic, but then, Kalliope had always been. Micah wondered if it was because she was so ancient, but he wasn't about to ask. The last thing he wanted was to offend her.

"Micah," she said as she paused just before reaching them. She was wearing sandals and heavy golden bracelets, earrings, and a necklace. The stones embedded in the jewelry were red like her dress.

"Kalliope," Micah answered, slightly bowing to her. It always paid to show her respect, something Verne didn't understand.

"I see you found my home. Who told you about this place?"

Micah wasn't about to tell her. It had taken him talking to

almost a dozen heroes to find out about this place, and he'd opened portals to three other temples before finding this one. "No one in particular. This place suits you, though. It's as beautiful as you are."

She cocked her head. "You were never so nice. Are you saying this because you hope I'll allow you to stay here and hide from the other conclave members?"

"I don't need you to hide me, just to listen to me."

She never looked at Constantine.

Micah was grateful for that, and that she had no idea how to work a phone. Even if she wanted Micah to be arrested, she wouldn't be able to make it happen quickly, not without calling for heroes. Her troubles with technology were one of the reasons Verne disliked her so much, but at the moment, it was an advantage for Micah.

"You have ten minutes," she said.

Micah understood how lucky he was that she'd given him even ten minutes. He took a step forward, but that was where he stopped. He didn't dare move any closer. He and Kalliope had both been conclave members until recently, but they'd never been friends, and she'd always intimidated him a bit. She was the oldest member, and there was something ancient in her that Micah had never seen in anyone else.

"There are rumors of you being present when the first conclave was created. I don't know if that's true, but even if it isn't, you know that the conclave was created to protect heroes, humanity, and the supernatural community. We were supposed to protect the innocent and help the heroes in their mission, but instead, Verne twisted that mission. He, Elmer, and Hester have been killing innocent people, *children*, people who only wanted to live their life. I always wanted that to change, but I wasn't able to do anything about it until recently."

"What did you do?" She sounded curious.

She must not know that Micah wasn't a conclave member anymore. Micah had to take a chance and hope it would work. "I've been working with the fallen heroes for several decades. I've been giving them information about the missions so they were able to save the innocent people our heroes were sent to kill. But Verne found out about me, and I had to leave. In his eyes, I'm a traitor."

"Which you are. You just admitted as much to me."

"I did betray the conclave, but I wouldn't have had to if it had been doing its job. Verne, Elmer, and Hester are using the conclave for their personal gain instead of what it was created for. It's not right, and something needs to be done about it."

"And you'll be the one to do so?"

"No one else stepped forward, so I suppose I will be. I already have Johnson and Claire on my side. When all of this is over, and the dust settles, you'll want to be on the right side, too."

Her dark eyes narrowed, and Micah half expected her to try to smite him. He wouldn't be surprised if she could control lightning or something like that.

"You want me to give up my seat on the conclave," she said slowly.

"I think that the only way to truly change things is to disband the conclave and create a new one. So yes. I'd like you to give up your seat and everything that goes with it. I'd also like for you to stand by my side so I can have the majority when deciding to put Verne and his friends on trial. Once the trial is over, no one will try to stop you from leaving. You'll be able to live your life the way you want to without having to answer to anyone." Micah suspected she'd always disliked having to tell Verne and the others what she did when she wasn't with the conclave. She was the only one who actually left the conclave building, and she disappeared for weeks at a time. Verne had always despised that, and they'd fought over it several times.

"I'll think about it," she said. "But it's risky."

"I realize that, and I wouldn't be here if I didn't need you. I'm not asking you to fight. You just need to be on my side and give me the majority so I can stand up to Verne, Elmer, and Hester. That way, you'll be remembered as one of the conclave members who stood up to the bad guys and saved many lives."

Micah prayed it would be enough to convince her, because if it wasn't, he didn't know what he'd do. He had to get the majority. Otherwise, his plan would crumble into dust before it even started.

Constantine waited until they'd left and Micah had called Mordred to ask the questions that burned his lips. "She's a character," he said.

Micah snorted. "That's an understatement."

"Can you tell me about her? I remember her from when I was a hero, but I don't think I ever had any real contact with her."

Micah bit his lower lip. "I'll tell you all about her, but first, I have a proposition."

That got Constantine's attention. "What kind of proposition?"

"Life has been hectic since I left the conclave, and that won't stop until the new conclave is in place. It could take weeks, maybe months, and I don't want to wait that long to go on my first date with you."

Constantine blinked. He hadn't expected Micah to want to go on a date, but he should have. It made sense. Micah had said he hadn't had a relationship in hundreds of years, since he'd become a conclave member. He'd barely even had flings, because he hadn't wanted to draw the attention of anyone on the conclave. Now, he and Constantine were together, but they hadn't gone on a date yet. They'd talked a lot, and they'd taken a lot of walks around the lake, but they weren't dates.

"What did you have in mind?" he asked.

"I have the perfect place."

"Well, I trust you, so take us wherever you want."

Micah's smile was blinding. He held out his hand and opened a portal, but instead of walking through it right away, he took Constantine's hand with his free one and pulled him along. Constantine went without resisting. He didn't have a reason not to trust Micah, and he was eager and curious to find out what Micah had in mind.

He blinked when they stepped out of the portal. They were in a small alley, and it took him a moment to understand where they were. Then he recognized the dark brownstones of the houses that were on both sides of them, and he grinned. A peek just ahead of them told him he'd been right and that they were in Amsterdam.

"Why here?" he asked.

Micah's smile was shy. "I've always wanted to see Amsterdam as it is now. I have been here, but that was when I was a hero, and it's been a long time."

"So it's the perfect first date," Constantine said with a smile. And now that they were here, he had something specific in mind. "Do you mind if I take the lead? I know the city better than you seem to."

"I trust you as much as you trust me."

Which was a lot.

Constantine pulled on Micah's hand and headed toward the canal just outside of the alley. The air was cold, but thankfully, it wasn't raining. The sky was turning dark, though, and he hoped to find what he was looking for from his memories.

"So, Kalliope," Micah said as they started walking.

"We don't have to talk about her on our date."

"But you were curious about her."

"I am. She seems like the odd woman out on the conclave. There are Verne, Elmer, and Hester, and from what you said, Johnson and Claire are their little group, though. Then, there's you, and finally, Kalliope."

"I can only tell you what I know about her, which honestly, isn't a lot. She's the oldest conclave member. No one knows her exact age, but I suspect she saw the Roman empire with her own eyes."

Constantine was stunned. All the heroes were old, because as long as they managed to survive their fights, they were immortal, but still. Kalliope sounded *really* old.

"I think that's why she stays away from the other conclave members. Not because she thinks she's special, but because she doesn't want to mingle with us youngsters. I'm the worst offender in that case, but she's never been rude, just standoffish. She's sided with me several times when I had problems with what the other conclave members did, which was why I thought she'd agree to help us."

"You think she will?"

"It's impossible to say, but I hope so. We need her. We can take care of the conclave even without her, but I'd really like to do this by the book. The conclave has been doing whatever they want for too long, and it's time to go back to the laws."

Constantine understood that point of view, although he wasn't sure he agreed. From where he stood, as long as the conclave disappeared, it didn't matter how it happened.

"She's not like Verne and the others," Micah continued. "But she's very self-serving, which I understand. The first person she thinks of is herself, and only after that, everyone else. I think that's one of the reasons she hasn't stood up to Verne yet. It wouldn't have benefited her."

The thought made Constantine angry. "The same goes for Johnson and Claire. I don't understand why they didn't want to help you. How can they stand by and watch what the others are doing?"

"You'd think that considering all of this, we have had the majority, but it hasn't always happened, and Claire told me that Verne is blackmailing her."

Constantine wasn't surprised. "What does he have on her?"

"I have no idea, and I didn't ask. It's none of my business. But as long as she and Johnson stand by me when I face Verne and his friends, I don't care. I was the first who broke the rules, after all. It would be hypocritical of me to point the finger at her."

"What do you think they'll do once all of this is over?"

"I suspect Kalliope would go back to her temple, or whatever place she lives in. As for Claire and Johnson, I don't know. I believe they'll disappear and that no one will see them again."

Constantine was glad that Micah had opened his portal where he had, because it meant they were close to the place he was looking for. He grinned when he saw it, and he pulled Micah along.

"What is this?" Micah asked as he looked at the boat in the canal in front of them.

Constantine dragged him close and wrapped an arm around Micah's shoulders. "Our first date. It's a dinner cruise on the canals."

Micah's jaw dropped open, and his eyes widened. "We can do that?"

The wonder in his voice made Constantine's heart ache. Micah was one of the strongest persons he'd ever met, and he'd done so much for the fallen heroes, but it had cost him. For hundreds of years, he'd put his personal life on the back burner. He hadn't dated, hadn't allowed himself to fall in love, and now, he found wonder in every little thing

Constantine did for him.

Constantine kissed Micah's jaw. "We can, and we will." No matter how much Constantine had to pay for it.

Luckily for them, the cruise wasn't crowded. They managed to get the best table in the rear of the boat. Constantine guided Micah with a hand on the small of his back as they climbed down the stairs into the boat. No one had said anything about them being two guys, but then, they were in Amsterdam.

Micah slid down the long bench and pressed close to the back window. With the sky darkening and the lights on in the boat, it was beautiful. Constantine hadn't chosen the city, but if he had, it wouldn't have been more perfect.

"Thank you," Micah said when Constantine sat next to him.

Constantine wanted them to be close. This was a date, after all, and even though he'd like nothing more than to watch Micah, he also wanted to be able to wrap him in his arms easily. That was why he'd paid a little extra to be sure they'd get the table in the rear. The seating was all on a long bench that curved around the table, and it was perfect for them.

"You have nothing to thank me for. You were the one who had the idea of a date."

"But I never imagined it would be like this."

"You like it?"

"It's perfect. That's why I was thanking you. For so long, I've had to lock away my personal life. I was afraid that if I got close to anyone, Verne would use it against me. It was lonely, and while I'm sorry I had to leave the conclave because it means I can't help the fallen heroes anymore, I'm also happy because it gave me this." He looked straight at Constantine. "It gave me you, and I couldn't have wished for a better man."

Constantine cupped one of Micah's cheeks and pulled him

closer, gently kissing him. "I'm happy I waited. I couldn't have wished for a better man, either."

Micah's chuckle was shaky as if he was trying not to cry. Constantine pulled him closer, twisting them so Micah's back was against his chest and Micah could look outside as the cruise began.

The boat was cute, in a touristy kind of way. The table was covered with a white cloth, and in the middle of it stood a red rose and a small candle. The bench was red velvet fabric, and thankfully, it looked clean enough. This table at the rear of the boat was kind of closed off from the others by windows, and even though they weren't alone, it gave them the illusion of privacy.

Constantine wanted Micah to be able to relax and have fun. He deserved this and so much more.

Micah didn't know what to say. When he'd asked Constantine to go on a date, he'd thought they would take a walk as they had so often around the lake. He hadn't expected the boat and the food, and he didn't know how to thank Constantine. He wasn't sure anything he could say would be enough.

They spent the entirety of the cruise pressed against each other, even when they had to eat. The food was nice, albeit not the best Micah had ever eaten, but he didn't care. It could have been a burger and fries, and he'd have been happy because he was with Constantine, and they were on a cruise on the canals.

It was magical. Micah had wanted to see Amsterdam again for decades, and it was one of his favorite cities. He was glad to see it hadn't lost its magic and even more so that he got to experience it with Constantine.

Micah had already liked Constantine before, but once again, he was surprised by how thoughtful the man was.

Micah had chosen the city they were in, but Constantine had made it work. Hell, it was more than that. He hadn't just made it work, he'd made it perfect, and Micah would remember this for the rest of his life.

He sighed when the cruise ended. He didn't want to leave, especially not to go back to their normal life, but it wasn't like he could lie down on the bench and sleep here.

"I'll take you on as many dates as you want," Constantine whispered in Micah's ear.

And Micah knew he would. He wouldn't make a promise he wasn't ready to keep. "Thank you for this," he said, feeling like he was repeating himself.

Constantine kissed Micah's forehead. "Stop thanking me. This was a pleasure both for you and for me."

And it had been. Micah was glad he'd asked Constantine on the date. They felt even closer than they had before, and Micah prayed he wouldn't lose this.

He couldn't believe that so soon after leaving the conclave, he'd found love. Constantine was perfect, and Micah never wanted to lose him. That meant he'd fight even harder to keep Constantine safe, but he was scared.

But that wasn't what he wanted to think about.

He and Constantine slid out of the bench and walked down the length of the boat. The captain greeted them with a smile and a little wave, and Micah waved back. Dutch wasn't a language he'd learned yet, but if he survived the fight with the conclave, he promised himself he would. If at all possible, he wanted Constantine and him to live here, although of course that, too, was something they'd have to think about later.

"What now?" he asked.

The night was dark, but people were still walking along the canals. Most of them were probably tourists, just like Micah, and it made him feel like he was part of something bigger.

"We should go home," Constantine murmured.

"I don't want this night to end."

Constantine's smile was wicked. "It doesn't have to end. We're going home, but I said nothing about us going to our respective rooms."

Micah swallowed. He couldn't remember the last time he'd had sex with anyone, let alone someone he cared about as much as he did Constantine. He was ready for this, though. He was ready for anything Constantine wanted to give him.

"Let's go home, then."

So they did. Micah opened another portal, and they quickly walked through it. They found themselves in the forest by the house, and even without talking, they didn't linger. Now that the promise of sex hovered between them, they both wanted to get to the point. Micah couldn't wait to find out what Constantine looked like without clothes, how he felt against his naked skin, and how beautiful it would be to wake up next to him tomorrow morning.

Even with the fight with the conclave menacing their future, this was the first step he and Constantine were taking in their relationship, and he couldn't wait to see what happened next.

Luckily, most of the people in the house seemed to be asleep. There were a few lights upstairs, and the living room light was on, too, but no one said anything when they walked past it. Neither of them stopped to peek in. Micah didn't care who was still awake. He only cared about Constantine, who was holding his hand and pulling him along the hallways and up the stairs.

Micah knew where Constantine's room was. He'd visited a few times, but beyond kissing, nothing had happened. Now, it would, and his body vibrated with anticipation.

"We don't have to do anything you're not ready for," Constantine said when they reached his bedroom.

They were still outside, as if Constantine was afraid that if he pulled Micah inside, he'd freak out. Micah had to show him that he knew what he was doing, so he pressed Constantine against the wall and kissed him. Constantine was slightly shorter, but his presence felt so big, almost as if he were trying to push his way under Micah's skin.

Their tongues tangled, and their teeth knocked together. Micah chuckled, but Constantine didn't let him step back. He tightened his hold around Micah's waist and kept him in the circle of his arms as he plundered his mouth the way Micah hoped he'd soon plunder his body.

He needed more. It had been so long since he'd last felt this way for someone, and while he almost couldn't believe Constantine was the one giving him this, he trusted the other man. Constantine wouldn't hurt him, whatever happened, whatever they did.

"Take me inside," he murmured when he was one second away from stripping Constantine in the hallway.

He doubted most of the fallen heroes would enjoy that. Hell, he wouldn't enjoy it, because he didn't want anyone else to see Constantine naked.

Constantine grinned. "I'm going to have to get to the door for that."

Micah took a step back, even though it felt like the hardest thing he'd ever done. He just wanted Constantine and to forget about everything else for an hour or, hopefully, for the rest of the night.

Constantine kissed Micah's cheek and turned to the door. He quickly unlocked it and pushed it open, but he hesitated before stepping in, blocking the way. "I didn't expect you or anyone to come around, so it might be a bit messy."

Micah had wondered for one second if Constantine was changing his mind, and he found himself laughing at Constantine's words. "I don't care if it's a dump. I just want you."

Constantine walked in, and Micah followed. After what

Constantine had said, he expected the room to be a mess, but it wasn't. It was wide, with windows making up almost the entirety of the wall furthest from the door. They opened on the lake, and it was an incredible sight with the moon illuminating it.

A massive bed occupied the center of the room. The fireplace in front of it wasn't lit, but Micah could imagine how warm the room would be if it were.

Constantine didn't turn the light on. He let Micah slowly move around the room, and Micah was grateful for that. He was overwhelmed by what had happened and what was about to happen. That didn't mean he didn't want it, but he was glad for the opportunity to take a breath.

There were two armchairs and a small table between them under the windows. Both the chairs were full of clothes, folded and not, and it made Micah smile. So that was the mess Constantine had mentioned.

When Micah turned to Constantine, it was to find him quickly picking up clothes and shoes from the floor and pushing them under the bed. Their gazes crossed, and Constantine sheepishly smiled.

"Sorry about that, but I warned you."

"You did, and I don't care about the mess. The view more than makes up for it." And Micah didn't mean the one out the window.

Constantine's cheeks flushed, a sure sign he knew what Micah was talking about. He stood there, looking as if he wasn't sure what to do. Micah had been the hesitant one, but their roles were reversed now, and Micah felt more secure. He was used to being in charge. Sometimes he could give it up with people he trusted the way he trusted Constantine. He didn't mind being in control, though, and it made him feel surer of his footing. This was the first time they were together, after all.

Still watching Constantine, Micah slipped out of his shoes. He slowly unbuttoned his shirt, making sure that Constantine's focus was on him as he moved only his fingers. He stroked his fingertips down his chest, opening the shirt until every button was released. Then he shrugged the shirt off his shoulders and added it to the pile on one of the armchairs.

Constantine groaned. "I'm sorry this place is such a mess."

Micah couldn't help but smile. "At least I won't have to look for the lube." Because a half-empty bottle of it was sitting on the nightstand.

Constantine hid his face in his hands. "This is a disaster."

Micah disagreed. He didn't care that Constantine's bed wasn't made or that shoes were still peeking from under the bed.

He took advantage of the fact that Constantine wasn't looking at him to unfasten his pants. They slid down his legs, and as he moved toward the bed, he shook them off his foot, almost stumbling as he did so. The sound made Constantine look at him, and his eyes widened.

"We had plans," Micah said as he snatched the lube.

"We did," Constantine croaked.

"Maybe you should start moving, then."

Micah dropped onto the bed and pushed the blankets down. He was still wearing his underwear, but it was easy to get rid of it, too. Once he was naked, he looked at Constantine, who seemed frozen in the act of pushing his jeans down his legs and was staring at Micah.

Micah dumped his boxer briefs off the bed and opened the lube. That seemed to get Constantine back into motion, although he almost fell on his face when Micah slicked his fingers and reached between his own legs.

"So we're doing that?" Constantine asked in a strangled voice.

"Unless you have a better idea?"

"Nope. No better idea. Everything is perfect." He paused and loudly swallowed. "You're perfect."

Micah could see he truly believed that. He was nowhere near perfect, but when Constantine looked at him this way, he could almost believe it.

He pushed a finger inside his body. He might not have had sex in decades, but that didn't mean he didn't take some time to himself. It wouldn't take him long to be ready for Constantine. Now, Constantine just needed to get with the program.

Constantine's jeans were still around his thighs, but he decided to take off his sweater. He got stuck halfway, making Micah snicker. Clearly, Constantine needed help, and Micah was more than happy to provide.

He slid his fingers out of his body and got to his knees. He quickly cleaned his fingers on the sheets, then reached for Constantine and touched his back. Constantine fought harder against his sweater as Micah guided him to sit down. He went along with it, and as soon as his ass was on the bed, Micah swung around and straddled Constantine's thighs. He helped Constantine untangle himself from the sweater and threw it behind himself.

He had Constantine the way he wanted him. He wasn't entirely naked, but Micah didn't want to wait anymore. He wanted to become Constantine's and for Constantine to be his.

He grabbed Constantine's face with his hands and kissed him. Constantine groaned and kissed back as he wrapped his arms around Micah's naked body. He tried to pull him closer, but there was only one way for them to be so even more than they already were.

"Fuck me," Micah whispered.

"I need to prep you."

"I already did. I'm ready for you."

Constantine stared at Micah for a second before nodding.

Micah was glad he didn't push or ask if Micah was sure. He'd never been more certain of anything, and he wanted Constantine to trust him on this.

Micah continued clutching Constantine as Constantine reached around him. Constantine's hand and arm brushed against Micah's naked skin, making him shiver. He wanted this man so much that he barely recognized himself, and he didn't even care. He wanted to be different. He wasn't Micah, the conclave member anymore, and he would never be again. In Constantine's arms, he was just Micah, and he loved that.

The head of Constantine's cock brushed against Micah's slick hole, making both of them hiss. They stared at each other as Micah pushed himself up just enough that he could then push down as Constantine held his cock up.

He held his breath as he did so. He should have prepped himself better, but he didn't want to wait, and besides, he knew that after the burning pain would come pleasure. Hell, there was some pleasure in the burning and in feeling Constantine slide into him as if he belonged there.

Constantine pressed his forehead against Micah's shoulder. His cock slid all the way into Micah, until Micah's ass cheeks rested on Constantine's thighs. Micah took a moment to enjoy the moment. Neither of them moved for a few moments, and it was perfection.

Then Micah had to move.

He raised his body, and Constantine looked at him. Constantine's cheeks were flushed, and his lips were parted as if he needed them to be open to breathe. Micah almost couldn't believe he was the one to make Constantine react this way. Constantine was kind and gentle and caring, and so, so beautiful, and he'd chosen Micah of all people.

Micah would always treasure that and the fact that Constantine had given him a chance. He was making Micah's new life so much better than Micah had expected or imagined.

They clung to each other as Micah moved. When Constantine started snapping his hips up as Micah pushed down, Micah knew it wouldn't be long for either of them to come, and god, he wanted that. He wanted to take Constantine apart and put him back together while Constantine did the same to him.

Constantine ran one hand up Micah's back, using the hold to keep him close while he kissed him. The kiss was openmouthed and messy, but it made Micah's body burn. He needed more.

His legs were cramping, but he didn't care. He rose up, then slammed down, helped by Constantine's hands on his hips and Constantine's movements. Constantine needed to come as much as Micah did, and together they worked toward that goal. The only sounds in the room were their panting and the slap of flesh against flesh, while the air smelled of sweat and sex — and them.

Micah hooked his arms around Constantine's neck and kissed him again. He could feel the pressure building in his groin, and he sobbed in pleasure when Constantine grabbed his cock. It wasn't the most straightforward position, but Constantine would make sure Micah came, too.

He came first. Between Constantine's hand on his cock and Constantine's dick in him, it was too much, and Micah couldn't stop the pleasure from taking over. He cried out and shuddered, pressing closer to Constantine as he painted their chests with his cum. He never stopped kissing Constantine, even when the kiss became little more than a panting press of their lips.

He squeezed his ass around Constantine, who pushed up into him one last time before burying his face against Micah's neck. Micah could feel his warm breath, and he held Constantine close as they both came down from their pleasure high.

"Will it always be like this?" Constantine asked as he rubbed Micah's back.

They were slick with sweat and semen, but Micah never wanted to move. He enjoyed feeling Constantine's softening cock in him, and he loved the fact that even when this was over, he'd be able to feel him. Constantine would be inside of him for the rest of the night and tomorrow morning. He'd be inside of Micah forever, not physically, but in Micah's heart.

CHAPTER NINE

It was time for the next step, and Micah was nervous. He, Mordred, and their supernatural allies had been through several video meetings, and though it had taken a while, they'd finally chosen who would sit on the new conclave.

Micah had been asked to take his place on the conclave again, but he'd refused, and before Mordred could stop him, he'd suggested him. Micah had no intention of ever sitting on the conclave again, and if he could avoid it at all, he hoped he'd never have to fight again once all of this was over. He wanted a peaceful life, possibly with Constantine.

He suspected several of their supernatural allies had been testing him when they'd offered him the spot. They'd seemed satisfied when he refused, and if it had been a test, he hoped he'd passed it. It hadn't been calculated, though. He had no interest in power or whatever else came with the new conclave.

"You could have chosen anyone else," Mordred grumbled on their way to his office.

Micah smiled. "But you're perfect. No one else would have been able to do this the way you will."

"I wouldn't be too sure of that."

"Well, you're a way better choice than me. You have ties in the supernatural community through Amyas, which is one of the reasons I believe that community has accepted you so easily. The fact that you haven't been a hero in hundreds of years probably helps, too. But it's Amyas's love for you that pushed them to agree you'd be good on the conclave."

"I still think I'll be shit."

"Which is one of the reasons you'll be perfect. Let's face it. The people who wanted to be on the conclave did a shit job."

Mordred's smile was wicked. "And the one person who didn't helped the fallen heroes take the conclave down."

"Exactly. Hopefully, there will be more balance now considering who the new conclave members are, but it also pays to choose the right people to begin with."

"I hope you won't regret it."

"I won't. I've been doing this for too long. I want to be free."

"But you don't think anything about me being stuck with this new conclave."

"You were born to do this. Of all the heroes who left the conclave, you're the only one who rose against them. You united the fallen heroes and the supernatural community. None of this would have been possible if you hadn't been you, and even though it comes with less freedom, I truly believe you'll do a great job on the new conclave."

Mordred grumbled, but Micah was convinced of what he was saying. He didn't know the other conclave members, but he did know Mordred, and they'd do a great job with him on it.

They reached Mordred's office, and once they were in, he made a beeline for his computer. He poked around for a moment, then gestured at Micah to come to stand next to him. That way, they'd both sit in on the meeting, and they'd both meet the other six conclave members.

Micah had names, and he knew which species the new conclave members belonged to, but he'd only met a few of them. He'd talked to everyone on the phone, but this would be the first time they'd be face-to-face, and it made him nervous.

He didn't have a reason to be. He was doing the right thing, as was everyone else. The new conclave members had been chosen by their communities, and they were representative of them. The same went for Mordred. Micah had expected either Tryg or Thor to become a conclave member, but instead, another draugr had been chosen.

And now, Micah was meeting all of them.

He looked at the computer screen. A few windows were already open, and Micah recognized Cassandra, the harpy he'd recently met. She nodded respectfully, and he mirrored the gesture.

The situation was odd. Usually, on these meetings, he had all the power. This time, though, he was the odd man out. He'd be the only one in the video call who didn't belong to the new conclave, and while it was a relief, it also made him wonder what was next for him.

Well, they still had to get rid of the old conclave, but once it was over, what would he do?

His mind flashed to Amsterdam. He wanted to go back, find a cute house, and settle down. He wanted to have his friends over for dinners, weekends, and vacations. He wanted to build a life that didn't have anything to do with fighting and giving orders, and he prayed he'd have the opportunity to do just that. There was a good chance he'd die in the fight with the conclave, but if he didn't, he'd do everything he could to make his dream come true.

New faces appeared on the screen. Thankfully, all of them were labeled with their names, and in a few cases, it was obvious which supernatural community they belonged to.

Haley was a leshy, like Dimitri. Dimitri had talked well about him, just like Thor and Tryg had talked well about Clay, the new draugr conclave member. Haley was a typical leshy, with green skin and hair, and Clay looked like he could be Thor and Tryg's brother, with his long blond hair and square jaw. They both nodded at Mordred, who nodded back.

The last three conclave members were Freya, Vesta, and

Elwood. Freya was a mage, and while Micah had never met her, he'd heard good things about her. Vesta was an undine, while Elwood belonged to the Fey people.

And together with Mordred, they were the new conclave.

"Welcome," Mordred said.

A few members wrinkled their noses, possibly at Micah's presence, but this would be the last time Micah was involved in this conclave. He and Mordred had both believed it would be good for him to talk to the members, but Micah wondered if they'd been right.

"I have to say I thought this was a joke until now. I didn't believe you'd truly answer," Clay said.

"I agree that the idea of a conclave made up of supernatural creatures is odd," Freya said. "But not the worst idea I've ever heard. If this can work, it will solve many problems."

"This *will* work," Micah intervened. "And it's not a joke." He cleared his throat and stood up taller. "As most of you know by now, my name is Micah, and I've been a conclave member for several hundred years. All this time, I've tried changing things from the inside. It wasn't enough, and I apologize for that. I couldn't save many of your people, and they died as a result of the orders given by the conclave I was a part of."

"And you don't think we should put you on trial and imprison you for that?" Elwood drawled.

Micah swallowed. This was something he'd known might happen, even as he'd hoped it wouldn't. "You could. If that's what the new conclave decides, then I'll stand trial."

"And I'll speak for him," Mordred said. His voice was harsh, and he was glaring at the screen. "Micah might have been a conclave member, but he's done everything he could to help us protect the supernatural community. He passed on information to us for years and let us know what the conclave was planning. His help wasn't perfect, but he did more for the supernatural community than many of you did. You protected your people, which is understandable, but what about the other communities? The fallen heroes were the only ones who protected everyone, with the help of Micah."

"And we're thankful for what he's done," Vesta said. "As for me, if he's put on trial, I'll vote for not guilty. He might have been a conclave member, but as Mordred said, we wouldn't be here today without him."

The other new conclave members started nodding, and Micah leaned against Mordred's chair. He was relieved he wouldn't have to face a trial. There was no way to know what the new conclave would have decided if he'd had to go through that.

"So, there's a new conclave, but what about the old one?" Clay asked.

"That's the reason behind this meeting. We need to talk about them and our plans to put them on trial and deal with what remains of their heroes." Micah straightened. He had this. This was what he'd been planning for years, and it was finally becoming a reality. He needed to keep his focus on the end goal. Everything that would come later would be a result of what happened during that fight, including his peaceful future in Amsterdam.

Constantine was bouncing on the couch as he stared at the TV screen. The living room was full of fallen heroes, all of them intent on watching what was happening on the screen. Constantine could hear excited whispers and a couple of worried ones, but he knew that everything would be fine once Mordred talked to them. The fallen heroes understood what was happening and that it was necessary.

"The conclave hasn't been doing its job in hundreds of years," Mordred said on the screen. His expression was harsh, and he looked almost regal, but then, so did all the other people on the screen. Well, except the one guy with blond hair and pointed ears who looked bored, which amused Constantine. How could the guy be bored with everything that was happening?

Mordred had sent a text to everyone to let them know that the new conclave would be recording a video and sending it to all the fallen heroes and heroes, as well as most of the supernatural community. It was odd not to see Micah on the screen with the others, but Constantine understood why that was. Micah had been in the meeting with Mordred, and he'd mentioned something to Constantine about that, but he was part of the old guard. This was something the new conclave had to do on their own, and they were damn good at it.

"They've been killing the supernatural community," Mordred continued. "They've been hurting the innocent people they were supposed to take care of. I know many heroes were taught that the only people they had to protect were humans, but that wasn't always the case. When have heroes started killing children? People who never did anything except want to live a peaceful life? That's what the new conclave is about. It has seven members, each of them belonging to a different supernatural species. That way, the community will be represented in a way it never has. Heroes will still operate under the conclave, but they won't be the only ones protecting the innocent anymore. Every supernatural community member who wants to train and learn how to protect their people will be welcome to fight under the conclave."

"But first, the old conclave will have to pay for what they've done," Cassandra—the harpy—said. "We have accepted the help of Micah, one of the old conclave members. He's been working with Mordred and his fallen heroes to take down the conclave, and finally, his plans have come to fruition. Together with the new conclave, he'll take down the old one, and a new beginning will start for the supernatural community. No one will hurt us anymore. As a new conclave member, I promise you that I'll always work for the good of my community of harpies and the supernatural community at large."

The other new conclave members nodded and murmured their approval of what Cassandra had said. Constantine's heart was racing. When they'd mentioned Micah, he thought something bad would happen. After all, Micah had been a conclave member for a long time. And even though he hadn't been okay with most of the orders given by the others, he'd had to go along with it. It was surprising that the supernatural community at large wasn't asking for his head, but then, Constantine didn't know how the meetings between the new conclave members and Micah had gone. Hopefully, they'd manage to protect him. After everything Micah had gone through, it was the least the new conclave could do.

"What we ask of you is hard," a lady said.

Constantine squinted, trying to read her name at the bottom of the screen. He could tell she was a mage from her red eyes, and apparently, her name was Freya.

"Getting to the old conclave won't be easy. We've made a deal with some of its old members so that the ones who are really responsible for all the death in the supernatural community will be put on trial. The problem is that they still have heroes working for them. That means that to get to the old conclave members, we'll have to fight, and that is what we're asking of you today. Anyone in the supernatural community who can and is willing to fight needs to contact the number on the screen. We'll need everyone's help to ensure this goes the right way. We won't rule the way the old conclave has. We won't force anyone into fighting, but we need your help."

"This is all bullshit," Bowen muttered from the other side of the room.

Constantine glared at him. He'd almost turned around and left when he'd seen his former best friend sitting on the couch, but he had as much right as Bowen to be here. If Bowen had a problem with him, he could be the one to leave.

But being here, sitting so close to him, had been awkward. Constantine had done his best to avoid looking Bowen's way, but now, he couldn't anymore.

"This is what we've been working for the entire time," he snapped. "We're taking down the old conclave. Isn't that the reason you're here?"

Bowen shot to his feet. "I didn't know these people would be invited to the fight," he said in a harsh tone. "And having a conclave made up of creatures? How is that supposed to work?"

Several people in the room sucked in a breath, and a couple of them got to their feet as if they expected to have to break up a fight. Constantine got up, too, but he had no intention of fighting Bowen. Still, he faced him, glaring at the man who'd once been his friend. "Is all of this because you're jealous?"

Bowen's cheeks flushed. "I'm not jealous." His tone held so much venom that Constantine was surprised he wasn't burning at the harshness of the words.

"Why do you have so many problems with the supernatural community then? It didn't used to be this way. You fought next to us to protect the innocent, no matter what species they belonged to. Yet now, you think this is ridiculous. What happened?"

"You know very well what happened. Yes, we should protect the innocent, but it doesn't mean we should mingle with them. We're too different. The supernatural community won't hesitate to stab us in the back if it benefits them."

Constantine looked around, wondering if anyone in the room agreed with what Bowen was saying. Thankfully, from everyone's horrified expression, he doubted that was the case.

"If this is what you really believe, I don't think you should be a fallen hero anymore. We've been protecting the supernatural community with the understanding that once they could, they would help us. *That* is what's happening. We're building a new future, and if you don't like it, you don't have to be part of it."

Bowen reared back as if Constantine had hit him. "You want me to leave?"

"I would have said no if you'd still been the old you, but you haven't been in a while. You've become angry and bitter, and I don't think it works well with the job you have to do. You should go before you say something you'll regret."

Bowen shook his head. "I knew this would happen when you started becoming friends with Percy, and see where this has taken you? You're so deep in with Micah that you can't see the truth in front of your face."

Constantine took a step forward. He wouldn't let Bowen talk badly about Micah, not when they were in private and not with people around them listening in to their conversation. Thankfully, Bowen seemed to realize that, and he started moving away. "You'll regret being on their side," he promised.

"The way I regret being on yours?" Constantine asked.

Yes, it was harsh, but Bowen deserved it. Whatever had happened to him, he wasn't the friend Constantine had been happy to have for decades. He would miss Bowen, but apparently, letting him go was the best thing Constantine could do. He already had enough to worry about with the old conclave getting ready for a fight and having to kill conclave heroes soon. Bowen was a complication Constantine couldn't afford — and didn't want to take care of.

CHAPTER TEN

Micah glanced around. The place looked good, even though it was still missing furniture, and it looked unfinished.

They'd needed to open their new office early because of the heroes leaving the old conclave behind. After the video they'd put out where the new conclave members had talked to their communities and explained what was happening, there had been an influx of heroes and members of the supernatural communities wanting to join the fight. To deal with so many people needing a place to stay and train, they had to rush through opening their new base, and while it wasn't fully finished, it was everything Micah had imagined.

And it wouldn't be his home.

It would be strange, but Micah could deal with it. He couldn't wait to be able to leave without looking back. He'd promised Mordred he would always be there if the man needed his help, but he doubted that would be the case. Mordred was a good conclave member, and Micah had no intention of ever sitting in on a conclave meeting again. That was his past, and he was looking forward to his future.

The future that was walking toward him with a bounce in his step.

Micah smiled at Constantine, who snatched him around the waist and pulled him close as soon as he reached him. They kissed, keeping it quick since they were in public, but it was what Micah had needed to face the rest of the day.

"Are you as busy as I am?" Constantine asked.

"I think so."

"Do you think you can take a few minutes out of your day to come with me? A few heroes just left the old conclave and want to talk to you. I think it would reassure them to see you."

Micah couldn't say no to that, not just because Constantine was the one asking. He understood how the heroes who left the old conclave felt. Many of them had believed that what the conclave was doing was wrong for a long time, but they hadn't dared leave before because they hadn't known they'd have a safety net. Now, they did, but they were being asked to work and fight alongside the people they'd been killing since they became heroes. It wasn't an easy position, both for the heroes and for supernatural creatures. There were tensions in the groups, and a few fights had already happened, but Micah hoped everything would smooth out.

They had to remember that they all had the same goal of finally taking down the old conclave. As it was, at the moment, the old and new conclaves operated side by side. Micah had made a quick call to Johnson yesterday, and Johnson had explained that Verne, Elmer, and Hester were pissed. They'd seen the video, and they'd sent out heroes to hunt the people who'd appeared in it and kill them. Thankfully, most of the heroes they'd sent out had instead decided to come to their side, and they were now in the building, trying to make friends with people they were supposed to kill.

It was a miracle there hadn't been more fights, really.

"Show me the way," he told Constantine.

Constantine grinned and grabbed his hand, pulling him along. He always did that, as if he was afraid that if he didn't hold Micah's hand, Micah would vanish from behind him. Micah couldn't say he blamed him. He was nervous, too, even though so far no one had tried attacking him. He wouldn't be surprised if it happened eventually, especially coming from a supernatural creature. There was a lot of pain in their community because of everything the conclave had done. And even though Micah had been working against the conclave, he'd still been one of them. No matter how hard he'd tried to stop certain orders, he hadn't been able to do anything.

Micah suspected that if Claire, Johnson, and Kalliope stuck around for too long, they'd end up having to appear in front of the new conclave. It would be better than it happening in front of the old one because it meant they might have a chance to survive. But the supernatural community wanted revenge, and Micah wasn't sure that the deaths of Verne, Elmer, and Hester would be enough. He'd managed to save himself, but he couldn't say the other three would be able to do the same. He wasn't worried for Kalliope as much as he was for Claire and Johnson, and he had a plan.

When the new conclave attacked the old one, Micah would warn Johnson and Claire. He'd need them, but he hoped he'd be able to give them enough time to leave after. He truly believed that if they managed to do that, no one would hear from them again, which would be for the best. Micah disagreed with some of the decisions they'd made over the years, and he couldn't say he liked what they'd done, but he didn't think they deserved to die. The only three who did were Verne, Elmer, and Hester.

But many people would disagree with him, which was why he'd have to be careful. There was no telling what would happen to him if someone found them out, which was why he had no intention of letting that happen.

"So, there are four of them in this room," Constantine said as they stopped in front of a door. "They relaxed when they saw me, but they'd like to talk to you. I guess that to them, you're still someone they look up to since you were a conclave member."

"I wish no one would look up to the old conclave," Micah

grumbled.

"I understand that, but for hundreds of years, the old conclave guided them. It's not something you can forget in such a short time. You just need to reassure them."

"I'll do my best." And hopefully, it would be enough.

Constantine opened the door and walked in, releasing Micah's hand. Micah cleared his throat and followed his man inside, curious about what he'd find there.

Like Constantine had said, four people were sitting around the table. There were several bottles of water and snacks on the table, but no one was eating. The four heroes were clearly too nervous to do so, and they jumped to their feet when they saw Micah.

The one closest to Micah gave a little bow. "Conclave member," he murmured.

Micah shook his head. "Micah, please. I'm not a conclave member anymore."

"That's going to take some time to get used to."

Micah smiled and took a seat at the table. "I understand that. But you've done the hard part already. You left the conclave and decided to be on the right side."

"What does it mean for us, though?" one of the women asked.

There were three women, plus the one man who'd bowed to Micah. Micah wished he'd thought of asking Constantine for their names.

"Whatever you want it to mean," he gently explained. "The new conclave doesn't expect anyone to do anything, including fighting. If you've had enough of this, or if you don't want to fight heroes you called brothers and sisters until recently, you're free to go. The new conclave won't try to stop you, and you'll be able to live your life as you want. No one will be forced to become a hero anymore or to work for the conclave."

"And if we want to work for the new conclave?" The man

asked.

"Then you'll have to follow the new rules. You'll have to work side by side with supernatural creatures."

"We thought that would be the case, considering the video."

"It is, and that's not the only thing that's changed. The new conclave has different rules from the old one. They allow relationships between the people who work for them, including heroes. You can be with anyone you want, be they a hero, a supernatural creature, or even a human. You'll be allowed to retire when you feel the time has come. There'll also be new jobs, including trainers and more diplomatic posts. With so many different communities working together, we need people for all of that. You'll be able to choose whether you want to fight or do something different within the conclave or even to leave."

"This sounds too good to be true," one of the other women murmured.

Micah smiled at her. "It does, but believe me, it's the truth. I've been working with the new conclave to make all of this happen, and even though I don't have any kind of authority anymore, I'll make sure that the heroes who leave the old conclave are safe and get what they want. We all sacrificed a lot over hundreds of years. It's time we get something in return."

That went for all of them, including Micah.

Constantine was glad to have some time with Micah. Like always when Micah spoke, he was in awe.

He understood why Micah didn't want to be a conclave member anymore, but he would have been a great one now that the conclave was on the right side of things. He hadn't had the opportunity to do so when he'd had to battle with Verne, Elmer, and Hester. And now he wouldn't be a part of it, but that didn't stop him from helping anyway.

Constantine could see that Micah had convinced the four heroes to fight on their side with just a few words. He'd managed to do what Constantine hadn't in an entire conversation.

"What if we decide to fight until the old conclave is gone, then leave?" Eliza asked.

She was one of the four heroes Constantine had been taking care of since this morning. They'd contacted the email that Mordred had put out with his first video, and since the location of the new conclave building couldn't be kept a secret, that was where Constantine had told them to go. Hopefully, they wouldn't betray them and let the old conclave know where it was, but it wouldn't change anything even if they did. The old conclave would be gone soon.

"That's another possibility," Micah said. "And we'd be grateful if you decided to do that. Even with the help of the supernatural community, it's going to be hard for the heroes to fight against people they once considered family. Besides, most supernatural creatures who are volunteering aren't fighters. They fought because they had to, but most would rather stay away from the fight. We won't force anyone to help, but we could use your swords."

Eliza and Michelle looked at each other. Constantine was pretty sure those two were together from the way they hovered close, as if they were afraid the other would disappear. He behaved the same way with Micah. With the old conclave, they would have been punished if anyone had found out. With the new one, people would be happy for them.

"We'll do it," Michelle said. "Eliza and I will fight the old conclave. I don't know what we'll decide to do once that's over, but I'm not saying no to sticking around for a bit."

"Thank you," Micah said.

"We'll stay, too," Matthew added. "After everything we've been through, I don't want the old conclave to get off easily.

If you need our help, you have it."

This was going even better than Constantine had expected. The heroes reaching out to them truly wanted to help. They weren't doing this because they wanted to find out what was happening and report to the old conclave. They'd known that what the conclave was doing was wrong all along, and now, they finally had a way to fix things.

Before, if they'd gone against a direct order or had refused to do what the conclave had ordered, they would have been punished. Constantine remembered all too well the trials and executions. The conclave had made sure that all of it was public so that no other hero would try to betray them. Heroes were strong, but not so strong as to go against the conclave and all the other heroes. For most of them, it had been easier to go on a mission and never come back. The others had continued obeying orders because they didn't have a choice.

And now, they did.

Micah spent a bit more time talking with them, but soon enough, they separated. Micah had things to do, just like Constantine, but when Micah headed out the door, Constantine rushed off after him. He snatched Micah around the waist and pulled him close to kiss him, not caring who might see them.

"What was that for?" Micah said in a breathless voice.

"You're incredible. The way you convinced all four of them to stay with us when I wasn't sure I would be able to do that was awesome."

"I'm sure you would have convinced them in time, too."

"Probably because I can be annoying when I repeat the same thing again and again. They'd have said yes just to get me to shut up."

That made Micah laugh. "You're not annoying. You're endearing."

"I'm pretty sure you're the only one who finds me endearing, but I'll take it."

Micah kissed Constantine again, but it didn't last long. With a sigh, he leaned back and pressed their foreheads together. He didn't seem to care who could see them, either, and Constantine loved that. He didn't want Micah to be ashamed of them being together, and he wasn't.

"I wish I had more time for you. I feel like since our first date, we've barely seen each other," Micah murmured.

"That's because we *have* barely seen each other." Constantine wrapped his arms around Micah. "Why don't you show me around this place? I've seen a bit, but not all of it yet, and I'm curious. I can't believe how quickly you managed to get it built."

Micah shook his head. "Not quickly. I bought this place several decades ago, and I've been fixing it up as I could over the years. Mordred and the fallen heroes have helped, too. I'm surprised you never did."

"I want to help now."

"You can." Micah stepped away and took Constantine's hand. "Come on. I'll show you around, then."

It was an excuse to spend more time with Micah, but Constantine was in awe of everything he saw around him.

The building was big, just like the one the old conclave was in. It needed to be, with so many people around, but the sights were entirely different. Before, there had only been heroes. Now, so many supernatural creatures walked down the halls that Constantine didn't know where to look. He recognized most of the species, but he almost asked a few what they were. The only reason he didn't was that he didn't want to offend anyone or to have to stop his walk with Micah.

The building had been planned differently from what Constantine had been used to. The new conclave didn't expect the heroes to live there, so while there were rooms where heroes could spend time, they were small and utilitarian. They could house heroes in an emergency or before and after a mission, but they wouldn't have to live there permanently.

And they really needed to find another word to describe the people who'd fight for the conclave. It wouldn't just be heroes anymore, but a whole group of supernatural creatures, and they deserved to be known as such. They were heroes, too, in a different way, but Constantine doubted that was what they wanted to be called.

He could see himself spending a lot of time in the gym if he stayed with the conclave once this was over. As he watched Micah explain where everything was and how he'd come up with the ideas, he wasn't sure this was what he wanted to do with his life anymore.

Micah's cheeks were flushed, and his eyes glittered. He moved his hands as he spoke, and the way he looked made Constantine want to kiss him. He was full of passion, and he loved what he'd done — as he should. It was incredible and not something Constantine had thought he'd see in his life-time.

But Micah wasn't staying. Once this was over, he wanted to start a life away from the conclave, and Constantine under-stood. The problem was that he wanted to be part of that life, and it wouldn't be easy if he also decided to stay with the new conclave.

Constantine had to think about this. He enjoyed protecting people, and he'd fought for a long time. With so many super-natural creatures joining them, he wasn't needed with the new conclave. If he wanted, he could retire, but what would he do then?

Although he was tempted to make it so, loving Micah couldn't be Constantine's only goal in life. No, if he wanted to be with Micah, Constantine would have to find something else to do. He didn't want to fight anymore because he didn't want the possibility of being taken from Micah. But hopefully, Mordred would need a personal assistant or something like that. Constantine had never dealt well with having to sit down for long periods of time, but he'd learn if it meant he could have everything he wanted — if it meant he could have Micah.

CHAPTER ELEVEN

Claire and Johnson were finally reaching out to Micah. Micah had half believed they'd decided to make a run for it and abandon him, so he was relieved to see both their faces on his computer screen when he answered the video call.

"I won't deny that it's a relief to see you," he said.

"I apologize for how long it took us," Johnson said. "We had to be careful. You know how the others are."

"I do, which is one of the reasons I didn't try contacting you again. How are the two of you?"

Claire and Johnson looked at each other. They'd clearly talked about this, and Micah held his breath as he waited for them to say whatever was on their mind.

"We'll help you," Claire said. "We can tell you when Verne, Elmer, and Hester will be here so you can have them arrested. You should be aware of the fact that they won't be alone, though. They suspect you're planning something, and they've surrounded themselves with heroes. They chose the ones they're sure are on their side, so you won't be able to convince them to back down."

"We'll fight them if we have to." Micah and the other fallen heroes weren't looking forward to fighting people they'd considered family, but it would be necessary. They'd reached out to the heroes many times. At this point, the only ones left with the conclave were the ones who believed in what the conclave was doing, and as such, it was better if they died in battle.

"We'll give you all the information we have, but first, you need to make us a promise."

Micah had expected this, too. "I'm listening."

"Now that you've put up a new conclave, Johnson and I know that we won't be welcome in this new group. We never expected that to happen, but we're worried that they'll put us on trial. We could have done a lot more to try to stop the others, but we didn't."

Micah couldn't deny that. "I've already talked to Mordred and the rest of the new conclave. I think that as long as you're gone when the dust settles, they won't try looking for you. They'll be too busy with Verne and the others."

"So you don't really need me," a female voice said.

Johnson and Claire both turned to face whoever had arrived. Micah recognized the voice, and he found himself smiling. "Kalliope," he said, inclining his head at her when she appeared on the screen.

She glared with her arms crossed over her chest. "You came to me to convince me to stand up against Verne and his minions, but you don't need me anymore."

"That's not true. I hope that by seeing that four members of the old conclave are standing up to the other three, some of the heroes still working for Verne will realize the truth. Plus, since Verne won't ever recognize the new conclave as such, the four of us need to show a united front. We're conclave members, and we've been so for hundreds of years. He won't be able to deny our majority. I want us to put the other three on trial and take care of them ourselves, but I'm not sure the new conclave will allow that. They want blood, and I can't blame them for everything that happened because of Verne and his minions, as you called them."

"What do you expect from us, then?"

"Just what I said. When I confront Verne, I need you to stand by my side. I need us to show Vernon that we have a majority on this. Hopefully, it'll be enough for the heroes to obey our orders to arrest Verne, Elmer, and Hester. They shouldn't be able to deny our orders when we have a majority of votes." Although of course, there was no way to know what would happen once the moment came.

"You're hoping for this to happen without any bloodshed," Johnson said.

"It's probably stupid, but yes."

"Well, we'll stand next to you, but I don't think it will be as easy as you hope."

"That's where the new conclave comes in. They'll support us if we need fighters. They're already putting everything in place, so that won't be a problem."

"Let me know where and when, and I'll be there," Kalliope said as she turned around to leave already.

"How should I contact you?" Micah asked before she could leave.

She wrinkled her nose. "I've turned on my phone."

That was an incredible concession for her—evidence for how seriously she was taking this. "I'll call you then," he promised.

There wasn't much else to say after that. Claire and Johnson told Micah what had been happening with the conclave, and he wasn't surprised to find out that Verne and his friends were kicking up a fuss. They wanted Micah to be replaced as a conclave member, but as long as Kalliope didn't show herself, they wouldn't be able to vote on it. Verne had always used the rules and the authority of the conclave to squash everyone under his heel, and now, he had to follow those rules.

Once the video call was over, Micah got to his feet and stretched. His stomach grumbled, and he wasn't surprised when he looked at his watch and saw that it was almost two in the afternoon. Once again, he'd skipped lunch, and Constantine hadn't been there to tell him to eat. He was working with the new fallen heroes and the many supernatural creatures who'd been joining them.

But Micah didn't need Constantine to be constantly by his side. He was still slightly uncomfortable in the house, but most of the people had been welcoming, if a bit distant. No one would say anything if he went to the kitchen and ate, so that was what he decided to do.

He made his way downstairs, wondering what he'd find in the fridge. Before he could reach the kitchen, though, a door slammed open, and Bowen barged into the entrance. He looked around. His eyes were wide and he was pale, and Micah could tell something had happened even before Bowen opened his mouth.

"There you are," Bowen said.

Micah took a step back. "What do you want?"

"It's Constantine. He's been hurt."

Micah sucked in a breath. "How? What happened?"

"He was training with some supernatural creatures, and he got hurt. Come on. He was taken to the infirmary in the new conclave building."

Micah followed Bowen outside. They had to open a portal, and to do so, they needed to be far enough away from the house. They rushed into the forest, and Micah's every thought was on Constantine. Had he lost him before they had a chance at a life together?

He didn't know what he'd do if that was the case. Even though they hadn't known each other long, Constantine had become a central part of Micah's life. Micah had thought they would finally be able to live their life once the old conclave was gone, but now, they might never have the chance.

"Come on," Bowen urged. He threw his hand out and created a portal.

Micah rushed into it without hesitation, blinking once he was on the other side. He looked around, not recognizing the place where Bowen had taken them. "This isn't the conclave building. Where are we?"

It was a forest, but not the one where they'd been standing just a few seconds ago.

Bowen was right next to Micah. He lowered his hand, and the portal snapped out of existence.

Micah was trapped. He could create a portal, but would he have the time to do that and run through it before Bowen grabbed him?

He stepped away from Bowen, trying to understand what was happening. "What have you done?" Had Bowen hurt Constantine?

Bowen grinned. "Nothing yet, but that's about to change."

"He won't love you because you get rid of me."

"Maybe not, but we're about to find out anyway."

Micah turned and tried to run. As much as he tried to keep up with exercise and training, he'd been a conclave member for a long time. He didn't stand a chance against Bowen, and trying to fight him would only get him hurt.

Bowen grabbed Micah's arm and pulled him back. Micah tried twisting around, but Bowen punched him on the side of the face. Micah stumbled and fell forward, barely managing to catch himself on his hands. Bowen took the opportunity to kick him in the stomach, and the birds in the trees around them flew away when Micah screamed.

He ended up on his back, staring at the sky. Bowen stepped closer, hovering over him for a moment before he pulled his leg back and kicked Micah straight in the head.

That was the last thing Micah saw before everything went black.

Constantine bounced on his feet as he reached the house. He remembered being in Melissa and Hannah's place, and he couldn't wait for them to get used to living with the fallen heroes.

He stepped into the house and waved at the foyer. "Ta-da."

The two women looked around. "It's impressive," Melissa said.

They'd reached out to the fallen heroes a few years ago, and they'd been working with them for almost as long, but they'd shared an apartment until recently. They wanted to be here for what happened next, and Mordred had given his okay. The two of them would move into two rooms here at the house until the fight with the conclave was over. Constantine didn't know what they'd do then, but he didn't know what he'd do, either, and he wasn't in a rush to find out.

He couldn't wait for the conclave to be gone and a new one to be in place, but at the same time, it was frightening. He'd been fighting against the conclave for decades and fighting in general for hundreds of years. What would he be if he couldn't be a fighter? He supposed he'd find out soon enough. Besides, Micah was in his life now, and Constantine had every intention of deciding their next step with him.

"Let me give you a tour," he said.

He kept it shorter than the tour he'd given Micah, mostly because the two women seemed overwhelmed. They'd probably need some time alone, but he made sure they knew where they could find food or anything else they might need while they were staying here.

The number of fallen heroes who lived in the house was increasing, maybe because the fight was getting close. Constantine loved living with so many people, but he knew not everyone was like him. He fed off the energy of people, but Micah, for example, needed time alone to relax and recharge.

They were different, but they worked together perfectly.

"And finally, these are your rooms," Constantine said once they reached the hallway where the two women would be staying.

He knocked on a door, then pointed at another door in

170

front of the first one. "You can choose whichever room you prefer, but they're similar. Each of them has a private bathroom, but one has a view of the lake, while the other gives on the forest."

The women looked at each other, and Hannah nodded. "I'll take the forest. The lake makes me nervous."

Constantine clapped his hands. "Great. Do you need anything else before I leave the two of you to settle?"

"I don't think so." Hannah hesitated. "But can we reach out to you if we need anything? I recognized a few heroes when we walked past them, but I'm still nervous."

"Of course. No one will have anything to say if you ask for directions. But feel free to call me. You have my number, right?"

"We do. Thank you, Constantine."

Constantine liked feeling useful. "It was a pleasure, and thank you for joining us in our fight."

Not all fallen heroes would be there. Everyone in the house had decided they would be. But some of the fallen heroes who lived on their own had stepped away from the fight. Constantine wasn't surprised. They'd found out what living away from the conclave and the heroes meant, and they didn't want to lose that. Thankfully, most of them had agreed to keep an eye on the rest of the country in case someone needed to step in, but they wouldn't have a role in the fight against the conclave.

"It's the fight of every single hero," Melissa said, sounding serious. "We allowed the conclave to do many things over the decades, and we shouldn't have. I'm glad we'll finally be able to put a stop to what they've been doing."

Constantine grinned at Melissa, then left to give her and Hannah time to settle down. He'd probably see them at dinner unless Micah had something else in mind.

The two of them had been spending a lot of time alone,

which meant they hadn't been with the other fallen heroes. Constantine didn't mind. He enjoyed being with Micah and finding out more about the man. For so many years, Micah had been a traitor and a spy. He'd focused only on that and had ignored everything else in his life, but now, that was over, and it was incredible to watch him settle and be comfortable in his new life. Constantine was proud that he was part of that new life, and he never wanted that to end.

So, he went to look for Micah.

The man wasn't in his bedroom or in the library. Those two rooms were where he spent the most time, so Constantine was at a loss. He decided to go to the kitchen, and if he couldn't find Micah there, to Mordred's office. Maybe they had a meeting Constantine didn't know about.

But he wasn't there, and neither was Mordred, so Constantine drifted to the kitchen. A couple of heroes were cooking dinner. Apparently, whatever they were cooking needed several hours in the pot.

"Have you seen Micah?" Constantine asked.

Lilith shook her head. "I haven't."

Constantine turned to go, but Marsha stopped him. "I saw him with your friend."

"Which friend? Percy?"

"No, the one who was your partner when you were heroes? I think that's what he said when we talked."

Marsha looked better now that she'd healed, and even though many people were awkward around her, she fit well. She was a no-nonsense kind of woman, and she'd started training the fallen heroes so they'd be in shape when the time came to face the conclave.

Constantine blinked at her words. "You mean Bowen?"

"Yes, him. I think they went outside? But I'm not entirely sure. This house is big, and I don't remember where everything is yet."

"I see. Well, thank you."

Constantine was frowning as he left the kitchen. Why would Micah and Bowen be together? Maybe they'd talked, and they'd finally made peace? It would be like Micah to do something like that, but not like Bowen. Constantine wouldn't have been surprised if Bowen held his grudge against Micah for decades.

But Marsha was sure they'd been together, so Constantine tried finding Bowen since he couldn't find Micah. His favorite places were the gym and the living room, but he was nowhere to be seen. Constantine ended his search at Bowen's bedroom door, pounding on it to get his ex-friend to open.

He didn't.

Constantine stared at the door for a moment, trying to wrap his mind around what was happening. What was going on? He couldn't be sure, and without Micah and Bowen, there was only one way to find out.

He turned around and rushed to the security room.

There were cameras all around the house, including in the forest area where most of them opened portals. Marsha had said they'd gone outside, and while it wouldn't make sense for them to go anywhere through a portal, at this point, Constantine was pretty sure that was what had happened. He couldn't find an explanation for it, but that didn't mean he couldn't accept it.

He almost collided with Bay as he turned a corner. Bay grabbed and steadied him, but Constantine was already pushing him away.

"What's going on?" Bay asked.

"I can't find Micah."

"Have you checked the library?"

Constantine almost snapped, but Bay was only trying to help. "I did. I checked the library, his bedroom, and Mordred's office. Then Marsha told me she saw Micah and Bowen together. I went to the gym and Bowen's bedroom, but he's not there, either. Both of them seem to have disappeared."

Thankfully, Bay didn't think Constantine was being dramatic. He nodded once, then let go of Constantine and turned around. "You were headed to the security room?"

"Yes. I thought I could watch the recording. Marsha said she saw them leaving the house, so maybe they're still around here somewhere? It's going to be easier to find them on the video than go outside and look for them."

Constantine was tense as they walked together. They didn't try to make conversation, and Bay didn't push Constantine to make sure he'd looked everywhere. He didn't seem to doubt that Constantine had, for which Constantine was grateful.

He was also grateful for Bay's presence. He was Mordred's second, and when he walked into the security room and ordered someone to pull up the videos from outside, no one argued. They did what he asked, and both he and Constantine leaned closer to one of the screens.

"What time?" the fallen hero at the desk asked.

"Can we go backward from now?" Constantine asked.

"Of course. You only want to see the area where we open portals?"

"To begin with."

Constantine stared at the screen. He sucked in a breath when Bowen and Micah suddenly appeared at the edge of the forest. They went backward. And once they disappeared toward the house, they raised a hand to stop the video. "This is what we need."

The fallen hero nodded and pressed play, and Constantine watched as Bowen and Micah rushed out of the house. The video wasn't great quality, but he could see Micah's eyes were wide and that he looked frantic as if something had happened. Bowen looked more relaxed, and together, they walked to the forest.

They never came back.

"Something happened," Constantine whispered.

He looked at Bay in the hope that Bay would tell him he was overreacting, but Bay's grim expression told him he wasn't.

Micah was gone.

Micah's head hurt. He knew exactly why, too. He remembered all too well that Bowen had hit him, which was why he stayed as still as he could, trying to understand where he was and if he was alone.

He couldn't hear anything or anyone else, just his own breathing. The air felt damp and cold, and the ground under him was the same. He was on his side, and to his surprise, his hands weren't tied. He slowly moved his fingers, trying to understand what he was lying on.

He was pretty sure it was stone, and it felt gritty, as if there was dirt on it. Between that and the dampness, it was easy to imagine he was in some kind of cell.

He waited a moment longer, but he could only hear his own breathing. Finally, he decided to open his eyes. He quickly blinked, then opened them only a sliver.

His cell was dark, but some light came from outside the door. It wasn't much because from what he could see, the door was wooden with only a tiny window in its middle. The window had bars, and he swallowed when he recognized the door and, with it, where he was.

A conclave cell.

He groaned as he sat up. His head throbbed, but he couldn't afford to whine about it. He looked around again now that he was more awake, and, sure enough, he recognized the cells under the conclave building.

He'd visited them too often. This was where the conclave put the heroes who disobeyed or went against orders. It was where they kept those heroes until the trial, then between the trial and their public execution. Sometimes they kept supernatural creatures here, too, but that didn't happen often. Verne and his friends would rather have the creatures killed than brought here unless they needed something from them.

Bowen had brought him to the conclave.

Micah wanted to scream and ask why, but he didn't have to. Bowen was angry, and he'd probably thought he was doing the right thing. Even if he wasn't, at least now, he had a clear shot at Constantine. Bowen didn't understand that Constantine wouldn't be with him even if Micah weren't in the picture. Constantine only saw him as a friend, and at this point, probably not even that. Besides, if Constantine found out what happened to Micah, he'd kill Bowen with his own hands.

Constantine was a happy-go-lucky guy, and he seldom got angry, but he cared about his friends and Micah. He wouldn't let this go, which was one thing that gave Micah hope.

Sooner rather than later, Constantine would realize Micah wasn't in the house. When he couldn't find him, he'd check the cameras. Then, he'd find out that Bowen and Micah had left the house together, and he'd know Bowen was involved in whatever was happening.

The sound of footsteps made Micah scramble back against the closest wall. He tried to get up, but his legs felt like jelly, and the pain in his head got worse. He groaned as the door opened, and since he couldn't get to his feet, he decided to stay where he was. At least here, whoever was coming couldn't attack him from behind.

He didn't know what was about to happen, but he'd worked with Verne for hundreds of years. Now that the man had gotten him back, he'd want to make an example out of him. He'd put him on trial, which meant that Micah had time.

The door swung open. The first to walk in was Bowen. And to Micah's surprise, he looked uncomfortable. Right behind him were Verne, Hester, and Elmer.

Verne was beaming as if it was his birthday and he'd gotten the best gift ever.

"Look who's back," he drawled.

Micah already knew what Verne would say, so he focused on Bowen. "Why?"

Bowen shuffled his feet. "You know why. You're a traitor."

"Of the conclave, not the fallen heroes. We both know why you did this, Bowen, and it's not because I betrayed the conclave. What do you think Constantine will do when he finds out about this?"

Bowen glared. "He won't find out."

"I'm pretty sure he already has, but even if he hasn't, you won't go back to him."

"Verne promised I could leave."

Micah snorted. Bowen had been so focused on getting what he wanted that he hadn't thought this through. "Verne has made many promises he never intended to keep. Look at where you are, Bowen. You're a fallen hero, and you walked straight into the lion's den." Micah would be surprised if Verne put Bowen on trial. He had enough to do with Micah, so Micah doubted Bowen would see the light of the next day.

Bowen seemed to realize that, too, and he turned, headed toward the door. Verne caught him before he could reach it.

The conclave member had a long knife hanging by his side. Micah had always believed it was mostly to scare the people around him, but as he watched Verne use the knife on Bowen, he realized the truth. Verne wanted to scare people, but he also enjoyed killing. The trials gave him satisfaction, but not the same as he was getting now, stabbing Bowen until the man fell on the cold ground. Blood pooled around Bowen's body, but he wasn't dead yet.

It took a lot to kill a hero, much more than being stabbed. If Bowen was left alone long enough, he'd eventually heal, but Verne had no intention of giving him the time to do that. He knelt next to Bowen's body, and Micah had to look away when he started cutting Bowen's head off. Unfortunately, that meant his gaze crossed with Hester's, who was wrinkling her nose as if Verne was doing something mildly annoying.

"How can you be okay with what he's doing?" Micah asked.

"Shut up," Elmer snapped.

Micah didn't miss the way he avoided looking at Verne. Apparently, neither Elmer nor Hester wanted to participate in what Verne was doing. That didn't make them better than Verne. They were enablers, and they'd pay for that and everything else.

"That was a nice way to start your interrogation," Verne said as he got to his feet. Micah avoided looking at the body. He hadn't liked Bowen, and he was angry at the man for what he'd done, but that didn't mean he had wanted to see him killed, especially not this way. Constantine would grieve his friend, and Micah felt sorry for him.

But he felt even more sorry for himself.

He knew what Verne and the others had in mind. They'd put him on trial, but as Verne had mentioned, they would interrogate him first. That meant torture, and while it was something Micah had trained to sustain, he knew that in the end, he'd break.

Thankfully, he and Mordred had planned for something like this. As soon as Mordred found out that Micah was gone, he'd put those plans into gear, and hopefully, Verne wouldn't be able to do anything to prevent what was about to happen to the conclave.

Verne came to stand in front of Micah. His clothes were

splattered with blood, and the knife he was still holding dripped on the ground next to him. There were drops of blood on his face, too, and it gave him a feral aura when he grinned. He raised the knife. "Ready for your interrogation to start?"

Micah didn't say anything. Nothing he could say would change the situation.

Two heroes came in, and together they dragged Micah onto a chair they placed in the center of the room. Micah had known Verne for long enough to be aware that this was his routine. He enjoyed torturing people, and while Micah had never gone through this, he'd been a spectator way too often. He knew what Verne was about to do, and he tried to steel himself for what was coming.

It didn't help.

Verne didn't ask questions. He didn't demand to know what Micah had planned, not yet. Instead, he slowly cut into Micah's forearms and chest, making sure to make it hurt as much as he could but without allowing Micah to lose so much blood that he'd faint.

The first few cuts were painful, but Micah powered through it. He lost count once they reached the twentieth, and by the time Verne stepped back, Micah was a sweaty and bleeding mess. He was shaking, and the fact that he knew this wasn't over by a longshot didn't help. He hadn't said anything yet because Verne hadn't asked questions, but he would start soon.

Verne stepped back, looking at Micah up and down as if he were staring at a painting he'd created. He grinned, then put the knife down and turned toward the small table that had been brought in earlier. Micah could see metal instruments on it, and he swallowed heavily, tasting blood.

The door slammed open, making Verne and Elmer jump. Hester cried out, retreating toward the back of the cell as if she expected to be attacked.

Micah blinked at Daniel. Where had he come from? What was he doing here?

"There's an emergency," Daniel said.

Verne glared at him so hard that Micah wouldn't have been surprised if he'd thrown his knife at Daniel's head.

"Call someone else. We're busy."

"I couldn't find someone else. This building is under attack."

Verne swore and moved toward the door. "Keep an eye on him," he ordered no one in particular. Then, he, Elmer, and Hester disappeared through the door.

Micah blinked, trying to wrap his mind around what was happening.

"Well? What are you two still doing here?" Daniel asked.

The two heroes who'd been framing Micah looked at Daniel. "He told us to keep an eye on him," one of them said.

Daniel rolled his eyes. "He wasn't talking to you. He was talking to me. Do you think he'd want the two of you to stay here when the building is under attack? Aren't you his personal bodyguards? Your job is to protect him, not to babysit a prisoner. Go on. I'll make sure this one doesn't go anywhere."

"Weren't you his personal assistant?" the other hero asked, gesturing at Micah.

"Not because I wanted to be."

They didn't seem convinced, but the sound of the alarm that suddenly started was enough to get them to move. They rushed out the door, leaving Micah and Daniel on their own.

Daniel peeked outside in the hallway. Then he rushed to Micah. "I'm sorry I didn't get here sooner," he said with a sob. "This is horrible."

"What are you doing?"

"What does it look like I'm doing? Come on. We don't have a lot of time before Verne and the others realize that no one is attacking the building."

Micah frowned. He felt like his brain didn't understand what Daniel was saying. "They're not?"

"I did all of this myself. I'm not staying here this time, though."

Micah wouldn't allow him to. After Verne found out about this, he'd have Daniel killed, and that wasn't something Micah could allow to happen.

As long as he was alive, he wouldn't let Verne hurt anyone else.

Constantine was freaking out. He needed to go out there and find Micah, but how? He didn't know where Bowen had taken Micah. There was no way for him to find out unless he got his hands on Bowen, but the man still hadn't come back. None of this made sense, and Constantine felt like his head was about to explode.

A hand clasped his shoulder and squeezed, making him jerk away. He relaxed when he saw it was Mordred, but not by much.

"We'll find him," Mordred promised.

"You can't be sure we will."

"Whatever happens, we'll find him. I doubt Bowen took him far. You said he was jealous?"

"Yes. He thought that if Micah wasn't in the picture, he and I would be together."

"Then he'll come back for you. Once he does, we'll ask him where Micah is."

"Mordred?" someone in the room called out. "Someone just opened a portal in the forest."

They were still in the security room, trying to find out what had happened, but as far as they'd seen, Bowen and Micah were the only ones in the video Constantine and Bay had already seen. Unfortunately, it gave no hint as to where Bowen had taken Micah.

Mordred turned, but Constantine was out of the room before anyone could stop him. He didn't know who was opening the portal, and it could only be someone who knew where the house was, but if it was Bowen, he had every intention of being the first one to greet him.

And what a greeting it would be. He'd strangle Bowen with his own hands if that was what he had to do in order to get answers out of him.

"Constantine!" someone yelled behind him, but he didn't stop to check who it was. He could disobey orders just this one. Surely, Mordred wouldn't hold it against him.

Constantine could hear people running after him, but he didn't think they were trying to catch him. They were running in the same direction he was, no doubt hoping like he was that Bowen and Micah were coming back and that all of this had been a horrible misunderstanding.

When he got out of the house, Constantine almost fell, but he caught himself on a low wall and continued running toward the forest. By the time he reached the area where the portal had opened, two people stumbled out of it. One of them was holding the other as if the second person couldn't quite stay on their feet, and Constantine cried out when he saw it was Micah.

He looked bad. His legs had folded, and the man next to him was holding him up and dragging him away from the portal. Micah was still wearing the shirt he'd put on that morning, but it was open in the front and on the arms up to Micah's shoulders, and it gave Constantine a full view of his bleeding chest and arms.

The portal flickered, then disappeared, leaving only Micah and the man supporting him there. Constantine finally reached them, ready to kick the man's ass, but his entire focus was on Micah when he got to them.

Constantine threw himself on his knees in front of the man he loved and reached for him, but he was afraid of hurting him.

"What happened to you? Who is this? Where's Bowen?" he asked.

"Give him space to breathe," the man said.

Constantine glared at him. "Who are you?"

"Constantine?" Micah asked.

Constantine turned his attention back to Micah. If this guy was a danger, the others would take care of him.

Constantine opened his arms, and Micah pushed away from the other guy and stumbled into them. He hissed, no doubt in pain, so Constantine didn't tighten his arms around him as he wanted. Instead, he moved Micah as gently as he could until he was in a position where Constantine could pick him up and carry him.

"What happened?" Mordred asked when he finally reached them.

Micah swallowed loudly. "This is Daniel. When I was with the conclave, he was my assistant, and he saved me. Don't mistreat him."

"As long as he's not the one who did this to you, we won't," Mordred promised. "Bay, take care of Daniel. Constantine and I will take Micah to the infirmary."

He didn't have to say it twice. Constantine started walking toward the house, careful of where he put his feet so he wouldn't jar Micah. It seemed like every move he made hurt the man in his arms, though, and Constantine winced every single time Micah whimpered.

"What happened to you?" Mordred asked.

"You can't interrogate him now. He needs to see the healer," Constantine protested.

"It's fine," Micah said. His voice was soft and tight with pain.

"It's not fine, and when I get my hands on Bowen, he'll regret the day he was born."

Micah sucked in a breath. "I'm sorry, Constantine. Bowen is dead."

Constantine blinked. He wasn't sure how that made him feel. He hated Bowen for what he'd done to Micah, but he couldn't ignore the fact that they'd been friends for decades. Bowen had been there for Constantine when no one else had, but things between them had changed, and the Bowen that Constantine had cared for wasn't the Bowen who'd died today.

"What happened?" Mordred asked again.

"Bowen took me to Verne. I don't know why he believed Verne would let him go, but he thought this way he'd get rid of me, and he'd be able to get Constantine. Verne had no intention of letting him go, though. He didn't even ask him about this house or the fallen heroes. He just killed him."

"He's dead?" Constantine asked.

"He is. I'm sorry."

"What about you? Was it Verne?" Mordred asked.

"It was. He hadn't started interrogating me yet, though, so I didn't tell him anything. This was just the beginning."

Constantine felt like he was about to cry. He'd always known Verne was the worst conclave member, and he'd attended several public executions. The heroes and supernatural creatures who died were never in the best of shape. Now that he thought about it, most of them had sported the same cuts Micah had on his chest and arms. That was obviously Verne's work, and Constantine found himself wishing that someone would do to Verne what he'd done to so many people.

"It doesn't matter even if you told them everything," Mordred said. "As long as you're okay."

Micah snorted, then winced. "I'm far from okay, but I'll

heal. Thanks to Daniel, they didn't get anything out of me. Verne was about to start interrogating me when Daniel came in and said the building was under attack. We almost got caught on our way out, but he created a portal and got us out of there. Once we were away, I created the portal that brought us here."

They finally reached the house, and Mordred opened the door. Several people were hanging around, and they all came to see what was happening. A couple cried out, and Constantine was pretty sure he heard someone sob, but he didn't stop to check what was happening. He needed to get Micah to the infirmary, and he needed to do it now.

"I'm fine," Micah said, gently touching Constantine's jaw.

Constantine glared at him, but there was no heat behind it. "How can you say that you're fine? You're bleeding, and you're so pale that I wouldn't be surprised if you were a ghost."

"Well, I'm not a ghost. It would take much more than this to kill me. I'll be okay."

"I love you," Constantine blurted out. Micah blinked at him, but Constantine didn't let that stop him. Now that the words were out, he couldn't stop them anymore. "I probably shouldn't tell you in this situation, but I thought I'd lost you. I don't want to wait anymore. So, I love you."

Of course, that was the moment they reached the infirmary. Jonah, the healer, was standing just outside the door, and he rushed toward them. He didn't give Micah the opportunity to answer, but that was fine with Constantine. As long as Micah knew how he felt, he'd gotten what he wanted. Now Micah needed to focus on healing and rest, and Constantine would be next to him the entire time, making sure no one bothered him and that nothing happened to him.

CHAPTER TWELVE

Jonah was already gesturing at Constantine to put Micah down on one of the beds, but when Constantine tried, Micah wouldn't allow him to let go. He grabbed Constantine's shoulders. "I love you, too," he said.

He didn't care how much his chest and his arms hurt. He needed Constantine to know.

Constantine's smile was dazzling. "You do?"

"How could I not?"

Jonah cleared his throat. "Gentlemen, the fact that you love each other is adorable, but I'd like to examine Micah."

That seemed to snap Constantine out of it. He nodded curtly and took a step back, but to Micah's relief, he didn't go far. He gave Jonah space to work on Micah, but he hovered next to the bed, ready to step in if Micah needed him.

That was one of the reasons Micah loved him. Constantine was so gentle and caring, and he gave Micah something Micah had never had. Micah wasn't ready to lose him, and he was even more sure of that now that he almost had.

He'd almost lost *everything*. If Daniel hadn't stepped in, Verne would have tortured Micah, and he'd have gotten all the answers he wanted out of him eventually. Then he would have kept Micah alive long enough to show him what he did with his friends and the people he considered family. Only then would he have killed Micah, and not one second sooner. The man was a monster, and as soon as Micah felt better, it would be time to fight him finally.

"Who did this?" Jonah asked with a growl. He was poking

at the cuts on Micah's chest, but no matter how gentle he was, it still burned like the pits of hell. "Verne."

"He always enjoyed his knives," Mordred murmured. He hovered nearby, looking like he wanted to ask questions.

Micah sighed. He might as well tell Mordred what happened. He would have to eventually, anyway, and the sooner he did it, the better it would be.

He cleared his throat. "Bowen came to find me. He said Constantine had been hurt. I was stupid enough to believe him, and I followed him. He promised he'd get me to Constantine, and since he was Constantine's friend, I didn't doubt his word. I should have."

Constantine stepped closer. He couldn't take Micah's hand, since Jonah and his helpers were working on both his chest and his arms, but he squeezed Micah's shoulder, silently letting him know he was there.

Micah needed that. He felt like an idiot, and he could have ruined everything. He wouldn't blame Mordred if his friend wanted to push him out. There was no way to know that Micah wouldn't do something stupid again.

"He knew you'd go with him if he told you I was hurt," Constantine said.

"I think he realized I love you. I followed him, and he knocked me out. When I woke up, I was in one of the conclave cells. I was alone, but that didn't last long."

"Who came to see you?" Mordred asked.

"The usual suspects. Verne, Elmer, and Hester. All three of them came, as well as Bowen. From what he said, Verne had promised he'd let him go if he delivered me, but of course, Verne didn't. When I pointed that out to Bowen and he tried to go, Verne stopped him."

Micah swallowed. He didn't want to go into details, especially with Constantine standing next to him. He looked at Mordred, and when Mordred nodded, he knew he wouldn't have to.

"Once he was done with Bowen, Verne turned his attention to me," Micah said. Explaining what happened meant Micah didn't focus on the pain. Jonah was working as fast as he could, but the pain and the sight of Micah's chest were a reminder of what Verne had done and what could have happened if Daniel hadn't stepped in.

"He didn't ask questions," Micah continued. "He used his knife on me, but he was about to move on to other instruments when Daniel came in."

"I recognize that name," Mordred said.

"He was my personal assistant. He stayed behind when I left, but I'm pretty sure he would have come with me if I'd asked."

"The fact that he stayed back was a good thing. He wouldn't have been there for you otherwise."

"It was, and he saved my life. He told Verne the building was being attacked, and when the three of them left, he convinced the heroes Verne had left guarding me to go with them. He even managed to rig the alarm so everything looked even more real. As soon as we were alone, he untied me from the chair and dragged me out. He created a first portal just as someone noticed us, and as soon as we were safe and away from the conclave building, I created the one that brought us here. I should have contacted you before bringing Daniel along, but I couldn't leave him there."

"You did good," Mordred said. "And I'm glad you're okay."

Micah's mouth was dry. "I almost wasn't, and I'm sorry. I'll understand if you ask me to step back."

"Why would I do that?"

"Because I didn't think. As soon as Bowen said that Constantine was hurt, I focused only on him. If I'd taken a moment to think about the situation, I would have known Bowen was trying to trick me. I risked all of us, and I shouldn't have."

Constantine's hand on Micah's shoulder tightened, but he didn't say anything. Micah waited, holding his breath as Mordred thought about his words.

Finally, Mordred shook his head. "I won't ask you to step away. This is your plan as much as it is mine, and honestly, I probably would have done what you did if Amyas had been the one in trouble. I'd do anything for him, and I wouldn't have hesitated if someone had come to me to tell me he was hurt. Don't blame yourself for this, Micah. You're human, just like everyone else here, and sometimes, you'll react like a human. This is what we've been fighting for, after all. We want heroes to be able to be human, have relationships, and fall in love."

Micah relaxed, as did Constantine. Mordred stayed just long enough to ask Jonah how Micah was doing. Jonah reassured him without giving him too many details, and Mordred eventually left to check in on Daniel.

"I can give you painkillers," Jonah said.

"I don't think I'll need them."

Jonah didn't look impressed. "No one ever thinks they will. Don't be an idiot—take them. I know what I'm doing, and if you want to be up to the fight when we finally face the conclave, I want you to do everything I tell you."

"He will," Constantine promised. "Even if I have to pin him down and throw the painkillers down his throat."

Micah found himself smiling. "I'll do what the doctor orders," he promised.

"Good." Jonah appeared satisfied. "Get as much rest as possible. You lost a lot of blood, so I'll make sure someone brings you something from the kitchen. The cuts are deep, and they'll scar, but you won't have any other signs of what happened to you. You're lucky your friend intervened when he did."

Micah knew he'd been. If Daniel hadn't been there, not only would he have died, but he would have done so after telling Verne everything he knew about the fallen heroes and their plans.

But he hadn't, and as soon as he was well enough, he'd be fighting the conclave like he'd been planning all these years. He wouldn't stop until Verne was dead and unable to hurt anyone else ever again.

And looking around himself, Micah knew he wouldn't be the only one.

Constantine was relieved when Jonah finally stepped away, leaving them alone. He felt like he was about to break, and he sat heavily on the plastic chair someone had brought close to the bed. He clutched at Micah's hand, and Micah clutched back as if he were afraid that if he didn't, they'd be torn apart.

"I'm sorry about Bowen," Micah murmured.

"You have nothing to be sorry about. What happened to him wasn't your fault."

"Maybe not, but I can see how much losing your friend hurts."

"I lost him a while ago."

And that was the truth. Constantine didn't understand how Bowen could have done something like this. His old friend wouldn't have, and none of this made sense.

How could Bowen have thought that if he handed Micah over to their enemies, Constantine would finally want to be with him? It didn't make sense. Bowen might not have known that Constantine was in love with Micah, but he'd realized how important Micah was to him. Yet, he'd handed Micah over to Verne and had allowed him to be tortured.

And he'd lost his life in the process.

"If it means anything, I think he truly cared about you,"

Micah said.

"Maybe he did, but he didn't care about me the right way. He wanted me to be his, and he didn't care what *I* wanted. He would have sacrificed you just to get his hands on me, and the thought makes me sick."

On the one hand, Constantine was sorry he'd lost a friend, but on the other, he was relieved Bowen wasn't in his life anymore. If he'd still been alive, Constantine would have kicked his ass so hard that Bowen would have tasted his foot in the back of his throat.

The Bowen that Constantine had loved as a friend wouldn't have done this. Constantine almost felt as if Bowen's love for him corrupted him, and he couldn't help but wonder if the same would happen to Micah.

Today, Micah had done something he wouldn't have done usually. He hadn't listened to his gut, and instead, he'd focused on Constantine and what might be happening to him. What if he'd died? It wouldn't have been Constantine's fault, but he would have felt guilty. He didn't want anyone to get hurt because of him, and while he realized that it was all Bowen's fault, he still felt guilty.

Would it be best for him to take a step away from Micah? What if something happened during their fight against the conclave, and instead of doing the right thing, Micah focused on him and got hurt? Constantine would never be able to forgive himself for that.

"Stop it," Micah snapped.

Constantine blinked. "Stop what?"

"Thinking whatever you're thinking. I can see the smoke coming out of your ears, and it doesn't look good."

Constantine sighed. One of the reasons he loved Micah was that the man didn't let him get away with anything. He could also read him better than Constantine could read himself, which, in some situations, was a problem. "You can't tell me that if you hadn't been with me, you would have gone with Bowen."

"Well, if I hadn't been with you, Bowen wouldn't have done this. Whatever you're thinking, I can think it, too. Maybe it would be better for you if I stepped away. If anyone knows we're together, you'll become a target, and Verne wants to hurt me. He'll do it through you, which isn't something I can live with."

Constantine glared. "You're not stepping away from me because of Verne."

"And you're not doing it because of whatever you're thinking." Micah squeezed Constantine's hand. "We're in love. Whether or not we work together, it won't change our feelings. Besides, Bowen is gone now. I doubt anyone else will tell Verne about our relationship."

"Bowen might have done so already."

"Maybe he did, and maybe he didn't. Whatever happens, we'll face it together. I won't allow you to push me away."

"I don't want to be without you, but I'm scared you'll get hurt." That thought hadn't left Constantine's mind since he'd realized what happened when Micah had vanished, and even though Micah was in front of him, he couldn't stop thinking about it.

Was this what being in love meant? Constantine had liked people, and he'd been in relationships, but he'd never felt like this for anyone else. It was terrifying, and he didn't know how to deal with it.

"And I'm terrified *you'll* get hurt. But don't you see? We might get hurt even if we're not together. How will you feel if something happens to me and we're broken up?"

"I'd be destroyed."

"Exactly. But together, we can be stronger. We can show Verne that love has never made heroes weaker, but rather, the opposite. We'll fight to protect each other, along with every fallen hero and supernatural creature who needs us."

"We will." Constantine couldn't say no to Micah, and he didn't want to.

Still, as soon as Micah had fallen asleep, he got to his feet and left the infirmary. He wanted to hit something, to get revenge for what had been done to Micah, and he couldn't do that if he stayed in the infirmary. Micah would be safe here. Jonah would keep an eye on him. And in the meantime, Constantine could go outside and scream at the moon or something like that.

"How is he?" a voice asked, startling Constantine.

He hadn't seen Percy was leaning against the wall by the door. "How long have you been here?"

"About an hour. How is he then?"

"He'll be okay. You could have come in."

Percy smirked. "I wanted to give you time alone. From what I heard, you finally got your head out of your ass and told him you love him."

Constantine rolled his eyes. "I did. But it's not like we were having sex."

"But you were taking care of him. And unless I'm wrong, you were talking. What happened?"

Constantine was surprised the entire house didn't know about this already. Or maybe they did, but Percy was being nice. "It was Bowen. He told Micah I was hurt, and Micah followed him. He brought Micah to the conclave, and Verne killed him."

"I'm sorry you lost your friend, but it was predictable. Bowen was an idiot."

Constantine found himself laughing. "He really could be sometimes."

"But Micah will be fine?"

"As long as he does what Jonah orders, he will be." And Constantine would make sure he did.

"Then focus on that. Unfortunately, there's no way for us not to get hurt with the job we do. With the fight ahead of us, we'll lose people, and while I hope it won't be anyone I care about, there's no guarantee. Don't waste time pushing Micah away. You'll regret it if something happens to him."

Constantine had half a mind to lock Micah in the infirmary when the time came, but he couldn't do that to him. Micah had worked to take down the conclave for so many years. He deserved to be the one to do it. "You're right," he said with a sigh.

Percy preened. "Finally, someone admits it."

"Don't let your ego get too big. I only meant that you're right this time, not every single time you say something."

Percy clapped Constantine's back. "I don't need to be right every time, just to hear you say it this once. Now, where were you going?"

"The gym. I need to burn nervous energy."

"Then let's go. That way, once you're back with your Micah, you'll be able to keep him relaxed and well-loved."

And in the end, that was all that mattered and all that was important to Constantine. He'd do everything he could so that Micah survived the fight ahead of them, and once they both did, to make Micah happy for the rest of their lives. Thinking that he could leave Micah was stupid, and he knew he never would as long as Micah wanted him.

And hopefully, he'd want him forever.

CHAPTER THIRTEEN

It was time.

Constantine was nervous in a way he hadn't been in a long time. This wasn't just a fight for humanity and survival. It would be a fight against people he'd considered family for hundreds of years. Some of the heroes he'd never met, while others he hadn't gotten along with, but they'd all been united by the fact that they were born heroes.

And now, they were about to kill each other.

Mordred paced by the fallen heroes. They'd gathered in front of the house and were waiting for him to give his orders. All of them had been briefed, so they knew what was about to happen, but it would be good to have their leader talk to them before they headed out.

Mordred finally stopped moving and faced them. He looked almost regal, with his air of authority and his serious gaze. He certainly inspired more loyalty and trust than Verne, Elmer, and Hester ever had.

"You know your orders," he said loud enough that everyone could hear him. "If at all possible, arrest as many heroes as you can. Those you can't arrest and who won't back down, you'll have to fight and possibly kill. When you find one of the three conclave members who are our targets today, restrain them. They won't go easily. They'll fight, and you might have to kill them. If that's what happens, don't worry about it. Either way, the old conclave will end today, and it will be thanks to us."

Everyone around Constantine cheered. He did so, too, but

he was nervous, and he eyed Micah from a distance. Micah wasn't in the ranks next to him but rather by Mordred's side.

He'd healed after what Verne had done to him. It hadn't been that long, just a couple weeks, and he hadn't gotten as much rest as Constantine wished he had. The past few weeks had been busy for everyone, but especially so for Micah and the members of the new conclave.

Hopefully, that busyness would soon fade. They were about to head into their fight against the old conclave, and hopefully, they'd win.

Micah had made Constantine promise he wouldn't focus on him, but Constantine wasn't sure he'd be able to keep that promise. He didn't know what would happen to him if something happened to Micah, but he could too easily imagine it, and it wasn't pretty. If he had to step in to save Micah, he would.

"I hope to see all of you back here later for breakfast," Mordred continued. "In the meantime, let's go."

He walked toward the forest, and they all followed him almost as one. Constantine lingered behind, and he noticed Micah did the same. They'd already said their goodbyes in their room earlier, but he couldn't just ignore Micah now.

"Nervous?" he asked when they reached each other.

They followed the others but at a slower pace. This was one time Constantine didn't mind if he was one of the last to arrive.

"More like scared, to be honest."

"I'm scared, too."

Micah pinned him with his gaze. "But you can't focus on me. Keep yourself safe, please. I would never forgive myself if something happened to you and it was because you were distracted."

"I can't promise I won't be distracted by you, but I'll do my best to keep both myself and you safe."

The corner of Micah's lips curled into a half-smile. "I suppose it can't get any better than that."

"Not if you don't want me to lie to you."

They reached the forest, where several portals had already been opened. They were attacking during the night, both because they hoped to take the conclave by surprise and because that way, most humans would stay out of the fight. Seeing so many portals illuminating the forest was odd and incredibly beautiful. They were one of the signs that many heroes were working together, something that Constantine hadn't been sure would happen.

They called themselves fallen heroes, but in the end, they were heroes, just like all the ones working for the conclave. They were born as brothers and sisters, and the conclave had corrupted that.

Micah paused in front of one of the portals. Constantine followed his lead, and they faced each other. His chest felt heavy, and he wanted to drag Micah back to the house and lock him up in his bedroom, but he knew better. Micah would never forgive him if he took him away from the fight, and he wouldn't forgive himself, either. No matter how protective he felt of Micah, no matter how horrified he was at the thought of something happening to him, it was his problem, not Micah's, and he'd have to learn to deal with it.

Micah gently touched Constantine's cheek. "I promise I won't put myself into unwarranted danger, and I'll do everything I can to come back to you."

Constantine grabbed Micah's hand and pressed his palm against his cheek, nuzzling against it before kissing it. "I promise the same. We'll have breakfast together in a few hours, all right?"

Micah's smile was more convincing this time. "We will." He leaned forward and kissed Constantine, but he didn't linger. As quickly as he'd kissed Constantine, he stepped away and turned toward one of the portals. He didn't look back as he stepped through it, and Constantine hurried after him.

There was no way to know what he'd find on the other side, and he held his breath as he stepped out of the portal and faced the place that had been his home for so long, and that now was little more than a place of torture and pain.

It was already a mess. From what Constantine could see, there had been several guards in front of the building. And as soon as the fallen heroes had started stepping through, they'd raised the alarm and had attacked. One of them was tied up to a tree in the parking lot, but Constantine could see several bodies lying on the ground, a sure sign that those heroes hadn't surrendered.

More heroes were streaming out the doors, and Constantine got ready for the fight. He took out his guns, knowing it would be better to take out as many heroes as he could with them before he had to resort to the sword. He quickly looked around one last time, but he couldn't see Micah anywhere, and since he'd promised he'd do everything he could to stay alive, he focused on the fight that was coming at him.

He shot the first hero in the leg. She stumbled and fell, crying out as she did so, but no one stopped to help her. The heroes coming behind her trampled her, making Constantine wince. He continued shooting, and even though Mordred had said to try to convince the heroes to surrender, there was no way Constantine could. The heroes weren't giving him the time to speak, and if he wanted to keep his advantage, he had to make sure they couldn't attack him, which meant shooting them in a way that would keep them down. Hopefully, they wouldn't die. Even a shot in the head might not be lethal, but Constantine couldn't make promises.

He tried to keep shooting at legs, but a few times, he had to shoot a hero in a more vital part of their anatomy, and he was surprised to see he didn't feel any guilt. He didn't want to kill anyone, but they were attacking him, and he was defending himself.

"We're in!" someone yelled.

By now, Constantine had taken out his sword. He had the gun in one hand, the sword in the other, but he couldn't continue this way. He swung his sword at an approaching hero, then raised his gun and shot him in the stomach.

He turned to see that Marsha was standing by the door and fallen heroes were streaming in. She was fighting with a hero, but it only took her a few moments to dispatch him. His body fell down the stairs, and he didn't try to get up.

Constantine rushed toward the door. By now, the fight had moved inside. When he stepped in, it was chaos. Heroes were fighting fallen heroes and supernatural creatures, with new ones coming in every second. There was a sudden flood of harpies, screeching and flapping their wings, and Constantine realized their allies had finally arrived.

That was why he hadn't seen Micah around. He and Mordred hadn't come here right away. They'd needed to pick up their allies, and now, they'd arrived.

It wasn't easy not to obsess over Micah's safety, but it became easier when Constantine had to defend himself and save his own life. He lost count of how many heroes he mowed down, or even where he was until he blinked and realized he was in the basement, where the cells were located. He growled when he realized that this was where Micah had been tortured. He didn't want to see the place, and there probably wouldn't be a way for him to identify the right cell anyway, but since he was there, he decided to free the prisoners. They probably wouldn't be able to help, but they'd be free, no matter what happened.

He peeked into the first cell, but it was empty. In the second, he found a hero, but she was unconscious. He made sure she wasn't tied up, and he left the door open in case she woke up, but there was no way to help her until the fight was over.

In the third cell, he found Bowen's body.

He stared at the body of who had once been his friend. Every inch of it was covered in blood, and the room stank of decomposition. It looked nothing like Bowen had when he'd been alive, and that helped a bit. Constantine had already made his peace with the fact that he'd lost his friend, but now that he had Bowen in front of him, he said a quick prayer. He wasn't sure he believed in god or anything like that, but Bowen had, and hopefully, he was at peace now.

Constantine turned around. He had work to do, and he had every intention of doing it. He owed it to himself, to Micah, and in a way, to Bowen.

"They're in the conclave room," Mordred said.

Micah groaned and wiped the sweat from his forehead. "Of course they are. Do we know how many heroes are inside with them?"

"Only a few. They rushed inside when they realized they were outnumbered, and we can't open the door."

"We're going to need explosives."

Mordred chuckled. "I figured, but I thought I'd talk to you first."

"Just grab it. It's not like we need to keep this building intact anyway." If Micah had a say in it, the building would be destroyed once this fight was over. He certainly had no intention of ever coming back if he could avoid it.

He and Mordred made their way to the conclave room. He'd spent hours in there, attending meetings and trying to convince the rest of the conclave to be on their side. He hadn't seen Claire, Johnson, and Kalliope yet, but they were somewhere in the building. He'd told everyone to let them be if they found them, and he hoped they hadn't freaked out and left because he needed them.

He looked up at the doors. Behind them was his past. His future was all around him—in the fierce expressions of the people standing next to him, in Constantine, who was somewhere in the building fighting for his life.

Micah pounded on the door. "Verne? We know you're in there."

"I'm going to kill you when I get my hands on you," Verne roared from inside.

Micah wasn't afraid. He'd never been afraid of Verne, and his torture hadn't changed that. Micah had healed, and he was stronger than ever.

He looked around. He was surrounded by allies, including all the new conclave members. They'd wanted to be here when this happened, even though they wouldn't be the ones to condemn Verne and his friends to death. No, for that, Micah would need the old conclave members, and he took his phone out. He ignored Verne's swearing and stepped aside, already calling Johnson.

"Where are you?" he asked when Johnson answered.

"The three of us are in my office. Someone tried to come in, but they didn't insist."

"I told everyone to leave you be. It's time for you to step in, though. Verne, Elmer, and Hester barricaded themselves in the conclave room. If we're going to condemn them to death, we have to do it now."

"We're coming."

Micah nodded, even though Johnson couldn't see him, and hung up. He turned to Mordred, who was talking to Freya and Clay, two of the new conclave members. Clay looked excited about playing with explosives, and Micah hoped he wouldn't bring the entire building down on their heads.

Mordred looked up when he felt him move closer, and he smiled. "They're coming?"

"In a few minutes. Have we solved the problem of getting inside this room?"

"Apparently, Clay knows explosives. He volunteered to blow up the door."

When Micah looked at him, Clay rubbed his hands. "It'll be great," he said.

"Will any of us be alive by the end of it?"

"Of course. I'm not an idiot. I can blow up the door and not damage anything else in this hallway."

Personally, Micah wouldn't have minded if Clay had done damage to the people inside the room, but it would be better if they carried out the executions the way they'd planned. The supernatural community needed to see their villains judged, and Micah was ready to help in any way he could. As a conclave member, this was his last decision, and he couldn't wait for all of this to be over.

He leaned against the wall as they waited and rubbed his face with his sleeve. There was a trace of blood on the garment when he lowered his arm, and he frowned as he touched his cheek. He couldn't feel any pain, so it probably wasn't his blood.

Tonight, he'd fought in a way he never had. Even when he'd been a hero, it hadn't been like this—fighting for the safety of the entire country. There had been a lot on his shoulders today, and he hoped he would be strong enough to carry that weight until he didn't have to anymore.

A hushed silence fell on the hallway, and Micah looked around. The fallen heroes and supernatural creatures that crowded the hallway parted to reveal Johnson, Claire, and Kalliope.

Johnson and Claire glanced around nervously, but Kalliope looked like a queen. She held her head high and walked as if she still owned the place, and Micah supposed that she did. They were still the conclave, even if it would only be for a few minutes.

The three of them stopped in front of Micah, and they all looked at each other. "Ready?" Micah asked.

Johnson chuckled nervously. "As ready as we can be. Will we be allowed to leave once this is over?"

"Yes. I already promised, and I don't go back on my promises." He looked at them in turn. "We didn't always see eye-to-eye over the decades, but working with the three of you was an honor."

Claire and Johnson shook Micah's hand, but Kalliope stared at it for a second. She curled her lips in a half snarl, but eventually, she did take Micah's offered hand. "I'll be happy never to see any of you again," she said.

Micah laughed. "I have to admit the same goes for me. I'm ready for all of this to be over."

"Then let's finish it."

Micah nodded and pounded on the door again. "Verne? I know you're behind this door and that you're listening. I need you to get Elmer and Hester."

"We're not surrendering."

"I didn't expect you to. But I have Kalliope, Johnson, and Claire with me. As I'm sure you can count, this is the majority of the conclave. We want to put your trial and execution up to vote. The same goes for Hester and Elmer."

"You can't do this." But Verne sounded hesitant in a way Micah had never heard.

"We sure can. And if you refuse to vote with us, we'll vote anyway. I just need the majority, right?" He was using Verne's rules against him, and it was so fucking satisfying.

Micah wasn't surprised when Verne stayed silent. He hadn't expected him and the other two to vote with him and the rest of the conclave. They knew how Verne, Elmer, and Hester would have voted, anyway. That was why Micah had needed the majority, and he had it.

He faced the other three again. "As a sitting conclave member, I'm aware of all the pain and death Verne has caused both heroes, humanity, and the supernatural community. We could put him on trial, but I don't think it's needed. I suggest we find him guilty of crimes against humanity. How do you vote?"

"Agree," Kalliope said in a strong voice.

"I agree," Johnson said after her.

Micah held his breath and stared at Claire. She was still nervous, but as he watched her, she raised her chin high and stared him in the eye. "Agree," she said.

Micah smiled. "With this decision, Verne will be put to death. Now, I find Elmer guilty of the same. How do you vote?"

The three agreed with him that both Elmer and Hester would be put to death as soon as they managed to get them out of the conclave room. Micah turned to the door again. "Did you hear that?" he asked Verne.

No one answered. It made Micah wonder what was happening behind those doors, but he wouldn't be the one to break in. He stepped aside and looked at Clay, who was waiting nearby with explosives in his hands, bouncing on the balls of his feet.

"As our last action as the conclave, we condemn Verne, Elmer, and Hester to death," he declared, hoping he was loud enough so that everyone in the hallway could hear him. "As soon as we can get to them, they'll be executed. We don't care how it happens. They do *not* deserve to be put on trial or to be given a decent death."

Mordred started clapping. It was awkward initially because it was only him, but that didn't last long. Soon enough, everyone in the hallway was applauding, and it made Micah want to run away. He wasn't proud of any of this. He'd done what he had to do, but now, it was over.

He wasn't a conclave member anymore. He was just Micah, and he was relieved to be able to step away when Clay moved closer.

He didn't miss the fact that Johnson, Claire, and Kalliope inched down the hallway until they were far enough away to slip out. Johnson paused and looked back, and when he raised his hand to give Micah a little wave, Micah waved back. He was pretty sure he'd never see any of the three again, and he couldn't say he minded. They'd done what they had to do, but it was time to focus on the future instead of the past, and Micah was eager to do just that.

EPILOGUE

Constantine and Micah made their way through the new conclave building. It was odd to see so many different people hanging around, walking and talking as if they hadn't been enemies until a few weeks ago. Micah supposed that the only real enemy had been the old conclave and the heroes who'd worked for them, but still. He was in awe at everything that had changed. And while he couldn't wait to finally be away from all of this, it was good to see that his hard work had paid off.

"You're sure you don't want me to stay with you?" Constantine asked, squeezing Micah's hand.

Micah smiled at him. "There's no need for you to. No one is going to hurt me."

"I didn't think they would. But I know you're not comfortable with the new conclave."

"It's not that I'm not comfortable with them. I just don't feel like I belong, and really, I don't. I don't understand why they need me."

"Because you have experience. As it is, you're the only conclave member still around. I understand why they wanted to keep you on speed dial as a consultant."

Micah had believed that once all of this was over, he'd leave it all behind. He should have known better. Not only did Constantine want to work with the new conclave, but the new conclave members needed Micah's help. They wanted to be able to contact him and ask questions, and Micah hadn't been able to say no. How could he? Everything that happened was partly his fault, and he felt it would take him a long time to make amends.

They paused in front of the wide door that opened into the new conclave room. The building was as different from the old one as it could have been, and Micah was glad. He didn't want the people who now worked and visited to be reminded of what the old conclave had done. This building was open to everyone, be they fighters or people who needed help, and it was light and airy.

"I'll go, then," Constantine said as they faced each other.

"You don't have to if you don't have anything else to do, but I doubt the conclave will do anything to me."

Constantine grinned. "Listening to you, it feels like they're trying to ruin your life."

Micah shook his head and kissed Constantine. "Come on. I'm sure they'll be happy to offer you a job, too." He took Constantine's hand and opened the door to drag him inside.

Constantine laughed. "But what about our house in Amsterdam?" he protested.

His voice faded as they took in the room. It was the first time either of them had seen it. And while it was similar to the old conclave room, Micah saw it differently. In this room, the conclave wouldn't be looking down at people. There was a wide round table in the middle, with chairs settled around it, facing the door. Most of the chairs were occupied, but the tension Micah had expected was nowhere to be seen. After going to so many old conclave meetings, Micah had expected it, but the new conclave members seemed to actually like each other, something he hadn't thought possible.

Clay and Mordred were talking, their heads close together, and Micah suspected they were plotting something. It was never good to give them too much freedom, and Micah was glad he wouldn't have to try to rein them in. It wasn't his job.

Cassandra was perched on the back of her chair, listening

to something Freya was saying and nodding as she did so. Elwood and Haley were looking at something on Haley's phone while Vesta had one earbud in and was bobbing her head to whatever music she was listening to.

Micah cleared his throat.

Elwood jumped and glared at him, then gestured at him to come closer. "Don't sneak around like that," he scolded.

"I didn't think I was sneaking. I'm sorry to interrupt this meeting."

Haley rolled his eyes. "It's our first official meeting, and to be honest, we have no idea what to do."

Micah had to resist the urge to smile. "Is that why you asked to see me?"

"It is," Vesta agreed. She'd taken the earbud out of her ear and had placed it on the table. "We're all a little lost here, except maybe Mordred. We have no idea what we're doing."

Micah looked around, found several chairs settled against the wall, and walked over to them to grab one. He hauled it up and placed it on the other side of the table. Constantine did the same, and together, they faced the new conclave.

If Micah was honest, they looked more like grumpy teenagers than a powerful conclave. They were as different as possible from the old conclave, and Micah believed it was a good thing.

He hadn't been quite sure what to do after the old conclave had been disbanded. He, Johnson, Claire, and Kalliope had voted for Verne, Elmer, and Hester to be executed. That had been the last official order they'd given, and the other three had disappeared after that.

Micah hadn't. He'd stayed and had watched as Clay blew a hole into the conclave room. Verne and his allies had been inside, along with four heroes who'd tried defending them. It had only taken a handful of moments for the heroes to be subdued, and by then, Elmer had committed suicide. Micah hadn't been surprised. He'd stayed out of it when Verne and Hester had been arrested, just like he'd stayed out of it when their death sentence had been carried out. It hadn't been his place to step in, even though he'd voted for it.

But since that had been the last vote of the old conclave, he'd given up the power to the new one. They hadn't wanted to make the executions public, and Micah had agreed. They hadn't needed to. Everything would be fine as long as everyone knew that the old conclave was gone.

And it was. Micah hadn't believed he'd be needed, but he didn't mind. At the very least, it answered his question about what he'd be doing next. He and Constantine had talked about moving to Amsterdam, and Micah couldn't wait to do that, but it felt good to have something to do other than romance Constantine.

"About that job offer," Mordred said. He raised a hand before Micah could say anything. "And yes, I know you believed you were going to retire, and you can. We won't force you to accept this job. But we talked, and we feel we need you. You're the only one who has any kind of experience as a conclave member. You refused to be a member of the new one, but we thought you could give us some tips."

Micah considered that. "So I'd be a consultant?"

"Exactly. This isn't going to be a smooth process."

"I agree it won't be, but I have no experience with this new conclave. I only know what the old one was like, and it's not something anyone wants to go back to."

"But you were the one who created this new conclave and the rules," Vesta said, leaning forward. "We don't expect you to vote with us or become a conclave member. I guess for me, at least, I'd like to have someone to call when I want to vent or when I have no idea what to do with a situation. This is a new world, not only for you but for all of us. Supernatural creatures never had a say in what happened, and now, we do, and it's a lot of responsibility."

"Which is why there are seven of you on the conclave." Micah looked at Constantine.

They should probably talk about this, but Constantine had expected this to happen. He'd been telling Micah just minutes ago. Micah didn't think he had to ask Constantine what he thought about it. Constantine's smile and slight nod were enough for him to know.

He turned his attention back to the new conclave. "I accept," he said.

Clay clapped while Mordred grinned at Micah. Micah didn't understand why everyone seemed so happy to be able to work with him, but he quite liked it.

He'd only ever wanted to help people and make changes. He'd had the possibility to do that by finally taking care of the old conclave, but he'd thought that was where it would stop. Instead, he was being offered a second chance. He wasn't a conclave member, and he didn't want to be, but he could still help the conclave do the right thing.

Which was all he'd ever wanted.

Constantine wasn't surprised when Micah agreed to become a consultant for the new conclave. He'd expected them to ask, and he'd expected Micah to say yes. He was proud of the man he loved, even though it meant they wouldn't be able to retire in Amsterdam.

Although that wasn't a bad thing. They had every intention of buying a house and moving there, but it would be good for Micah to have something to do beyond exploring the city and learning Dutch. Constantine knew Micah, and he was aware of the fact that Micah worked best when he felt needed. He had to work to change things for the better, and now, he would.

And Constantine was so fucking proud of him.

"We have a job for you, too, Constantine," Mordred said.

"I'm not fighting anymore. I've done enough of that," Constantine said.

But Mordred knew him. "Not fighting, no, but what about training? You were so good with the heroes who left the conclave to work with us that everyone here thought you could be one of the beginner trainers."

"What does that involve?"

"You'll be given the newbies, so a mix of new heroes and supernatural creatures who have no idea how to fight. You'll have to get them into shape so other trainers can take over, and I think you're the best man for the job. People feel comfortable with you, and that's what will be needed for the people who join us."

Constantine looked at Micah. He'd expected Micah to have a job with the new conclave, but not himself.

Micah took one of Constantine's hands and squeezed. "You'd be a great teacher," Micah murmured.

"What about our plans? Amsterdam?"

"I don't see how this job would change our plans. We'll still go home to Amsterdam once the day is over, but since we have eternity to be together, it will be good for both of us to have something to do."

And Constantine wanted to say yes. He didn't want to fight anymore, but this wouldn't be fighting. This would be spending time with people, getting to know them, and as Mordred had said, getting them into shape.

Constantine could do that.

"All right. I'll be a trainer," he told Mordred.

He didn't stick around for long after that. Being with the conclave was Micah's job, not his, and he had nothing else to say to the conclave members. He liked that they were much more friendly than the old ones had ever been, though. When he said his goodbyes, every single one of them shook his hand and told them they were happy he'd accepted the job. Micah moved as if to come with Constantine, but Constantine pushed him back in his chair and kissed the top of his head. "This is where you belong," he whispered. "Talk with them for as long as you want. I'll find something to do."

And he did.

After exploring the new building, he found the cafeteria and grabbed a sandwich. He'd noticed Bay and Percy were sitting at a table, so he made his way toward them. He hadn't seen them much since that night at the old conclave building. Everyone had been so busy they'd barely had time to text, let alone talk in person.

Percy beamed when he saw Constantine. "There you are. I was wondering how long it would take Mordred to rope you into accepting a job for the new conclave."

Constantine laughed. "You, too?"

Percy waved between him and Bay. "Both of us, actually. Bay is going to be the contact person for all new and old heroes. I'm a trainer."

"Weren't they afraid you'd kill the new fighters?"

Percy's grin was wicked. "That's why Mordred said he didn't assign me to the newbies. I have the experienced fighters."

"That's better. I got the newbies."

"And you'll be great with them. They need to be mothered, and you do that really well, from what I remember."

"And aren't you glad I mothered you until you gave in?"

"We certainly wouldn't be here if you hadn't." Constantine leaned back in his chair and looked around. It was hard to believe that, after all these years fighting, they'd finally gotten what they'd been working for. It would take a while for the new conclave and its fighters to get in shape. But many of the heroes who'd worked for the old conclave had agreed to work for the new one, at least for a while. It was good to see those heroes mingling with supernatural creatures, and even though there was still some wariness, it would fade.

Constantine stayed at the table with Bay and Percy for a while until he noticed Micah walking into the cafeteria. He was talking with Mordred and Clay, and the smile playing on his lips told Constantine they'd done the right thing by accepting the jobs they'd been offered. He couldn't wait to get some time alone with Micah and to find a home they could call theirs, but they couldn't be each other's everything. They both needed something to do, and now, they did.

But Micah was Constantine's future, his everything. He was the one thing Constantine was never giving up. And when Micah turned and their gazes clashed, he knew the same went for Micah.

Everything around them had changed, and even they had. But their love would always be there, growing and shifting along with the changes of their new lives.

ABOUT THE AUTHOR

Catherine is the creator of several series, most of them paranormal, including the Whitedell Pride Series and the Gillham Pack Series. While she graduated in translation, she decided to go the writer's way because it was more fun to create her own stories and characters.

She's been living in Italy for more than twenty years, but she's a daughter of the North—Belgium to be precise—and she misses it so much that she's already planning to move back.

She loves pizza—probably too much—her son, her pets, and of course, books. She sneaks some reading time into her schedule every time she has five minutes free from writing, demands from her various pets and son, and lastly, housework.

Connect with her:

lievens.catherine@gmail.com
BookBub: https://www.bookbub.com/authors/catherine-lievens
Website: https://authorcatherinelievens.com/
Facebook: https://www.facebook.com/catherine.lievens.9
Facebook Group: https://www.facebook.com/groups/411788002341528/
Twitter: https://twitter.com/authorCLievens
Newsletter: http://eepurl.com/c-uvKn